D0301906

6
FEET
DEEP
ROSE IMPEY

700038817792

6 FEET DEEP

ROSE IMPEY

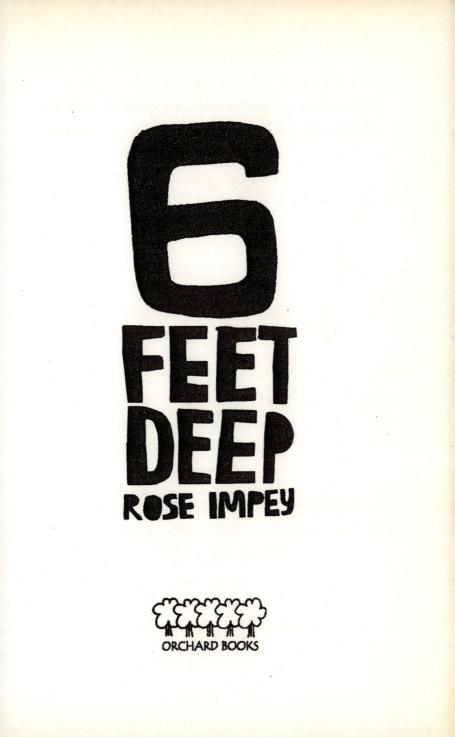

ORCHARD BOOKS

For Catherine
With thanks to Geoff Smith, Dave Goodall and CASF,
Darren Coe, Eddie See and all the schools I rely on.

ORCHARD BOOKS
338 Euston Road, London NW1 3BH
Orchard Books Australia
Level 17/207 Kent Street, Sydney, NSW 2000

First published in 2009 by Orchard Books
ISBN 978 1 84616 285 5
Text © Rose Impey 2009
The right of Rose Impey to be identified as
the author of this work has been asserted by her
in accordance with the Copyright, Designs and Patents Act, 1988.

All rights reserved.

A CIP catalogue record for this book is available
from the British Library.

3 5 7 9 10 8 6 4 2

Printed in Great Britain

Orchard Books is a division of Hachette Children's Books,
an Hachette UK company.
www.hachette.co.uk

He was blindly wriggling in the dark, like a worm. Soil – and all the unimaginable things that might be in it – filled his ears and his nose and whenever he tried to snatch a breath it filled his mouth too, making him choke. The panic left him dizzy. Not that he was in any danger of falling; he was already deep underground and desperately trying to dig his way out.

A worm, he thought bitterly, would at least have some sense of which way was up and which was down. He could be digging himself even deeper. What other choice did he have but to dig on in terror, scrabbling with his fingers and sobbing with frustration?

Then, just when he thought his lungs might burst, he suddenly broke the surface, gasping and shuddering, less like a worm now, more like a fish on a hook.

CHAPTER ONE

Jordan was awake, lying in a tangled mess in his bed, sweating and shivering – his only conscious thought to stop the terrible noise.

He leaned over the side of his bed, groping around in the pile of clothes that lay where he'd stepped out of them the night before. He rummaged in the pocket of his jeans, searching for his mobile, wondering how long it had been ringing.

'Good morning, sweetheart!' his mum's voice rang out, brightly. 'How are you this morning?' Jordan rolled back into bed and covered the phone while he tried to clear his throat.

'Jordan Gibbons! Are you not up yet?'

''Course I'm up,' he lied, but his still-croaky voice was a bit of a giveaway.

'You haven't had that dream again, have you?'

'No,' he snapped. 'I just couldn't find my phone.'

'As long as nothing's wrong...'

Wrong? What on earth could be wrong? he thought bitterly. He was being woken for school by his own mother, calling him on her mobile from a box six feet under the ground more than a mile away, where she had *chosen* to be buried alive. Now what, he was tempted to ask, could *possibly* be wrong with that?

But Jordan was under strict instructions to *do* nothing – and to *say* nothing – that might upset his mum, especially now that she was so close to setting a new world record. So he resisted the temptation and stayed silent.

'Well, it's Friday,' his mum reminded him, 'so don't forget you've got swimming. I think it might be raining so take your coat, and *please,* Jordan...have some breakfast? Dad says you're skipping it most mornings.'

Jordan really didn't have time for this. The truth was he should have been up half an hour ago. 'Gotta go, Mum, you're breaking up,' he said.

His mum's reception, from six feet under the

ground, was poor, and always gave him a good excuse to get off the phone.

'Hang on, sweetheart. I need some shopping. I want some toothpaste, a *TV Times*...oh, and will you get me a...*crackle...crackle...*'

'I can't hear you!' he shouted down the phone.

'A packet of prunes,' she shouted back. 'Those no-soak ones.'

'When am I supposed to do that?'

'Oh, well, if you're already late...'

'I am not *late*,' he insisted, getting up at last. 'See you in a bit.'

Jordan turned off his mobile and threw it onto the bed. He *was* late, and if he wanted to avoid another detention he really would have to get a move on. He tossed yesterday's clothes onto the mound already festering in the corner of his bedroom. He knew that was the word his mum would have used – if she'd been there: a *festering* heap of dirty washing. But she wasn't there, and what she didn't know couldn't hurt her.

Since it was the end of the week his choice of school shirt was either a grubby worn one or a clean one with a hint of green to it. His dad wasn't great at the washing and hadn't mastered the art of separating whites from coloureds; Jordan's PE kit was an embarrassing shade of pink.

He made only the briefest visit to the bathroom, but going to school without gelling his hair was unthinkable. Jordan took a lot of stick from his brother, Kyle, who took delight in flattening his carefully constructed hairstyle and calling him *a girl*, but Jordan didn't care. He couldn't see why girls should be the only ones to bother about their hair.

At the bottom of the stairs he gingerly opened the kitchen door and braced himself for his morning face-licking. Despite his size, Jet was still only a puppy, and his joy at seeing Jordan every morning almost made up for his mum's absence. That was the reason why they'd got the dog in the first place – as a distraction for Jordan. But his dad had made it very clear that a dog came with responsibilities.

'He'll be your dog. It'll be up to you to do all the walking, training and cleaning up after him. I shall be far too busy supporting your mum.'

And for the first few weeks, having Jet *had* been a great distraction for Jordan. The walking, even the cleaning up, Jordan still managed brilliantly, in his opinion. But he'd have been the first to admit that the training wasn't exactly going to plan.

'Down, *down*, boy,' he told Jet in a stern voice, then immediately undermined his authority by making a huge fuss of the dog in return.

When Jet was finally calm enough to let him into the room, Jordan grabbed a half-eaten packet of biscuits and reached for the dog's lead. This only worked Jet up even more, and it took all Jordan's strength to get himself and the dog outside the house. It was raining, but hardly enough to warrant going back for a waterproof, and he set off round the block at a trot.

The morning dog walk was another thing Jordan hadn't really time for today. But, unlike a shower and cleaning his teeth, this job couldn't be skipped. Jet would be in the house all day on his own and they couldn't afford any more accidents. The whole way round, Jordan tried to coax Jet to *please do his business*, but, as if sensing Jordan's desperation, the dog refused to co-operate. He'd done plenty of wees, one against every lamppost they'd passed, but the more critical *number two* remained elusive. In the end Jordan had to return home hoping the dog would manage to hold it until he got back at four.

Jordan grabbed his bag and found some money his dad kept in the cutlery drawer specifically for his mum's shopping. He closed the door securely to keep Jet in the kitchen, then pulled the front door behind him, instinctively patting his pocket to check he'd got his key.

Before he'd even reached the street corner he remembered his swimming gear and his maths homework, which he still hadn't done! Jordan raced back into the house. Jet, ecstatic at the prospect of a second face-licking so soon after the first, threw himself against the kitchen door until Jordan was obliged to open it to calm him down again. On the fridge he caught sight of his dad's daily update: *132 days down, 18 days to go!*

As he raced up to his bedroom, Jordan did the sums – four months gone, less than three weeks to go, which meant only two more weekends without his mum. Since the beginning of December everyone had been telling him that the end really was in sight now, but eighteen days still felt interminable to him and the prospect filled him with rage. This time when he left the house, he slammed the door so hard the windows rattled in their frames.

Finally, he was on his bike, on his way to school, via the shop to get his mum's shopping and collect his best friend, Anand. He recited the list in his head to make sure he didn't forget anything: *TV Times*, toothpaste, *prunes*! Jordan almost spat out the word in disgust. He did *not* want to know that his mother was constipated *again*. How many other boys of thirteen were intimately acquainted with their mothers' bowel movements? But then, how many other boys had a mother prepared to be buried alive – just to get into *The Guinness Book of Records* – just to win back some stupid record her own father had set thirty-odd years ago?! Only Jordan. He was quite sure that no one else belonged to such a weird and demented family as his.

Privately, Jordan feared that this was the kind of loony behaviour he could look forward to himself when he grew up. He briefly wondered if there was such a gene as '*an obsessive desire to be buried*' gene. If there was, he prayed he hadn't inherited it.

Jordan passed two of his neighbours standing talking by their cars. When they saw him, the women turned and gave him the familiar look – one that seemed to say: *oh, the poor boy, what can his mother be thinking of?* Jordan wondered the same thing daily, but he wasn't going to let his neighbours see that. He rode slowly past, giving them a cheery wave and smiling happily until he was out of sight, then he swore under his breath and pedalled for all he was worth. To be late for school today, after his recent warnings, would be really asking for trouble.

His form tutor, Mrs Raynsworth, had been sympathetic in the early weeks. 'We all know this can't be easy for you, Jordan,' she'd told him. Back then he'd still been one of her favourites. 'The blue-eyed boy', Jordan's friends used to call him – or sometimes *the Fixer*, because whenever anything went wrong, Jordan could always be relied on to come up with a plan to fix things, to get them all out of trouble. But Jordan was coming to realise that things weren't always fixable, and that his credit with his form tutor was fast running out.

'Your home situation,' she often now told him, 'isn't an acceptable excuse for lateness, poor work, bad behaviour and missed homework, Jordan. It's certainly not *a licence to skive*.'

Funnily enough, back in June, when Jordan had first told his friends about his mum's world record attempt, *a bit of a skive* was exactly what they'd predicted it would be.

'You lucky devil,' Anand had told him. 'Just imagine: nobody on your case morning till night…going to bed when you feel like it…'

'Never having to tidy your bedroom...' Martine added.

'Just pleasing yourself... Man, I'd swap with you any day.'

'Me too,' Martine agreed. 'What I wouldn't give for a five-month holiday from my mother! Especially if she took my sister with her!'

Jordan himself had never believed it would be a picnic, but at least for the first few weeks there'd been some pluses: he'd got a dog, he'd enjoyed a bit of fame at school, he'd had his picture in the papers a few times – even been on TV. But the novelty had soon worn off. Now all he got were stupid wisecracks at school – *Here come de Undertaker* or *It's the Son of the Mummy* – and endless warnings at home: *Don't rock the boat, keep your head down, don't do anything to upset your mother...blah! blah! blah! blah! blah!*

Turning briefly into the main road, Jordan saw his sister waiting for her bus to work. He really missed Chrissie since she'd left home. Instinctively he waved to her, but she was with a couple of her friends so he wasn't surprised when she looked the other way. He tried not to take it personally. He knew it wasn't him she was angry with.

He rode down Anand's street, reciting the three things his mum had asked for: toothpaste, a *TV Times* and the dreaded ✳✳✳✳✳✳ prunes. When he reached the shop Jordan went inside, already turning red at the thought that anyone from school might see him buying them. How his mother went to the toilet, in a box not much bigger than a coffin, was the burning question everyone wanted to ask, and he was deeply sick of the subject.

Anand's dad was behind the counter; his mum was filling shelves at the back of the shop. Anand was just back from his paper round. The two boys cocked their heads and Jordan said hello to Mr Solanki.

'Good morning, Jordan,' he replied. 'How is your mother? Still surviving, I pray.' Jordan nodded. Mr Solanki bent towards Jordan and added confidentially, 'I must say, Jordan, I am very much worried about your poor mother's safety.'

Me, too, Jordan wanted to say, but he just nodded instead.

'These people who flock to visit her...they are checked thoroughly, I hope. There are so many disreputable people around, so many crackpots, to say nothing of the terrorists lurking around every corner.'

Jordan quickly shared a smile with his friend. Anand described his dad as a merchant of doom. In his view, his father watched too many news programmes and read too many papers. But it had been discovering the internet that had really been his undoing.

'He thinks every new person that comes into the shop has some dark motive,' Anand said. 'He's OK with the locals, but he watches strangers like a hawk in case they're carrying a bomb, or planning to hold us up at gun-point. *I do not know what this world is coming to*,' Anand mimicked his father. '*The world has gone stark staring potty.*'

'I look at the internet,' Mr Solanki confided in Jordan now. 'It is full of the most shocking things. Do you have the internet, Jordan?'

Jordan shook his head. They didn't have a computer at home, now his sister had left and taken hers with her. When his mum went underground it had been a choice of a new computer or a dog – a no-brainer as far as Jordan was concerned. Of course there were things he'd use the internet for, if he had it: information about fishing, mainly – but he could live without it.

'No, we don't have it,' he mumbled.

'No, well, there is more than enough on it to keep

a person awake all hours of the night,' said Mr Solanki. 'I think it is a very mixed blessing in disguise.'

Jordan smiled and went to find the things he needed. He returned to the counter, trying to hide the prunes under the *TV Times*. When Mr Solanki put them through the till he gave Jordan a sympathetic smile, but said nothing.

Anand, his *so-called friend*, on the other hand, called out across the shop, 'Your mum bunged up again?'

Jordan shot him a warning look and was shocked to see Anand secretly filling his coat pockets with chocolate bars. Anand was concealed from his father by the free-standing shelves of sweets, but Jordan instinctively looked to see where the CCTV cameras were pointed. Of course, he realised, Anand would know exactly where to stand to avoid them. Jordan looked down, anxious not to give his friend away, but outside the shop he quickly tackled Anand. 'Are you mad? What you playing at, nicking all that stuff?'

Anand just laughed and held out a selection of chocolate bars, fanned like a pack of cards. 'Take your pick,' he grinned.

'Won't your dad miss them?' Jordan asked with some concern – not too concerned, though, to take a Mars Bar for himself.

'Nah, he don't count the sweets. Ciggies are a different matter. I can only get away with the odd packet.' Anand flashed one before returning it to his pocket.

'Since when did you smoke?' His friend was a mass of surprises this morning.

'They're not for me, twit,' Anand laughed, but before Jordan could question him further he raced off on his bike and Jordan had to struggle to catch up with him.

When the boys reached the fork in the road, instead of heading for school, Jordan turned his front wheel towards the track that led to his Uncle Matt and Aunt Julie's farm and market garden.

'We're gonna be late,' Anand warned, but Jordan waved the shopping bag, then rode on.

'You're the one who's gonna cop it,' Anand called after him, still hesitating. But in seconds he'd overtaken Jordan and the two boys battled it out up the hill to the car park, doing spectacular skidding stops on the gravel, stones spraying in all directions.

Immediately, a window opened in the nearby bungalow and his Aunt Julie's voice rang out loud and clear. 'Jordan, don't you rush off. I want a word with you.'

CHAPTER TWO

The market garden and self-pick farm that belonged to Jordan's Uncle Matt and Aunt Julie was called The Pick of the Crop. The car park looked out onto strawberry fields, but now, in early December, there was no crop to pick. On the edge of the first field, conveniently adjacent to the car park, was the spot where Jordan's mum was buried. A hundred metres away was his aunt and uncle's bungalow, beyond it the market garden, and beside that a new wooden building that housed a café and gift shop. This had been opened to take advantage of the crowds that were flocking daily to visit his mum.

Jordan wondered why anyone was prepared to pay

good money to stand gawping down a tube: the same tube through which his mum's meals and other daily needs were lowered down to her. It wasn't like they could see anything; Jordan himself hadn't had so much as a glimpse of his mum in four months. If it hadn't been for the photos and videos at home, by now he could easily have forgotten what she looked like.

It was obvious that she must be having the same problem, because she kept asking for particular photos from home, which she Blu-Tacked round the walls of the box she was buried in. Jordan still had to remind himself to call it a *box*, and not a coffin, especially around his dad. It was one of the things he was very touchy about.

For a month before she began the record attempt, *the box* had been in his mum and dad's bedroom and she'd spent all day, every day, in it, practising. It had made Jordan feel as if he was living with the Addams family. What made it seem even more bizarre was the fact that the box had tiger stripes all over the outside of it. It had been specially made for his mum by a local packaging firm whose logo was a tiger!

The box was bigger than a coffin, but not much, and still not big enough to actually sit up in. It measured a little over two metres by seventy-five centimetres, by seventy-five centimetres. Inside the box his mum had a mattress and a pillow, a miniature TV, her iPod and a lamp – nothing else, apart from her photos and a notebook. She was supposedly keeping a diary, although Jordan couldn't imagine what she found to write in it.

'It isn't as if she's *doing* anything down there,' he grumbled to Anand, as they parked their bikes.

'She must be bored out of her skull,' Anand agreed.

'You'd think. But she says there's no time to get bored; there're always too many people wanting to talk to her.'

When his mum was first buried, back in July, there had just been a patch of rough ground with a little bit of decking and a few garden chairs for visitors to sit on. His mum had been able to see the sky when she looked up, and the stars at night. But as it got a bit cooler, and her visitors started complaining about feeling cold, or wet if it rained, Jordan's uncle and dad had put up a shelter. It was a wooden lean-to, a bit like a long bus shelter, and they'd bought a couple of patio heaters too. It made it quite cosy, his dad insisted. He spent most evenings reading to his wife from the local paper, or just sitting companionably in silence after the crowds had gone home.

They'd all thought that the number of people coming to visit would tail off after a while, but the opposite had happened. Soon they'd had to install a turnstile to control the crowds. Now there was a sign telling people, *20p for two minutes with the woman in a box*.

It made Jordan feel strange having a mum who was a kind of local freak show, but when he'd complained she'd said, 'Why should you care, if I don't? If I'm going to be down here anyway, we might as well make some money out of it.'

The money that was made from the shop and café went to his uncle and aunt, but the money that was taken on the turnstile all went to charity. There was a large notice-board keeping a running tally of the number of days she'd completed and the days she still had left to set a new world record.

Jordan's grandfather had first set the record in 1967. He'd been continuously buried for one hundred days. Twenty years later, an American had overtaken his record, managing 141 days. Jordan's mum had easily beaten her own father's record way back at the beginning of November. In just over a week, on 12 December, if all went well, she would beat the American's record too and set a new world record of her own. Altogether she had pledged to stay down there for one hundred and fifty days to create a clear margin between them.

'Not much longer now,' Anand said, following his friend as he climbed over the turnstile.

Jordan nodded, then called a warning to his mum. 'Look out! I'm sending down your things.'

Attaching the shopping bag to the hook that was permanently set up for the purpose, he began to lower it down one of the two tubes. They were the size of large drainpipes. This first one, at the head end, was to allow his mum's meals and other things to be passed down; the other at the foot end was to aid ventilation. A fan was permanently running because, to Jordan's surprise, even though it was now winter, keeping his mum cool had been the biggest challenge.

Slowly, Jordan lowered the bag until he felt his mum lift it off.

'Thanks, Jordie,' she called back, and he retracted the wire.

His little cousins, Rosie and Ruby, had christened the device *hook-a-duck*. They'd spent hours sending their toy farm animals up and down in a plastic ice-cream bucket, until one time they'd filled it so full it had got wedged in the pipe and there had been a massive panic until they'd got it free. The girls weren't allowed around there unsupervised any more.

'Hello, Mrs Gibbons,' Anand called down.

'Hello, darling. How are your mum and dad? Remember me to them.'

'Will do. By the way,' Anand said, cheerily, 'if those prunes don't do the trick my nani ma has the same problem and she uses this stuff that looks like bird seed but she swears by it. It seems to help it all slide out...'

'Oh, God!' Jordan groaned, almost sickened. Anand grinned back; he had quite a fascination with lavatorial stuff.

'Look, we've gotta get to school, Mum,' Jordan called down.

'Yeah, don't you be late,' his mum told him. 'Come back later, though, and stay for a bit longer, eh?'

'Yeah, maybe,' Jordan hedged. 'If I don't get a detention,' he added under his breath.

He vaulted the turnstile and turned to pick up his bike. Anand was already on his. Jordan checked his watch. They might just make it, by the skin of their teeth. But any hopes of avoiding a detention were dashed at the sight of his Aunt Julie coming towards him. She held Ruby by one hand – Rosie must be getting ready for school – and a plastic ice-cream bucket in the other containing his mum's breakfast.

'You'd better go on without me,' he told Anand. 'No point us both getting a detention.'

His cousin ran over and waved her current favourite soft toy under Jordan's nose. 'Say hello to Dogalog.'

'Hello, Dogalog,' Jordan said, as ordered. 'I'm late for school already,' he told his aunt, but she ignored this, looking him up and down and shaking her head in despair.

'If your mother could see you now she'd...'

'Turn in her grave?' Jordan suggested, flippantly.

'That's not funny, Jordan. I was going to say she'd be even more worried than she already is. You don't look like you've been near a bathroom in days, which won't help your eczema, and those clothes look like they've been slept in.'

Jordan let it all drift over him, but even the mention of his rash made him automatically start to scratch. He hoped she'd get to the point soon and then he could escape.

'Your dad says you're not eating any breakfast.'

'I was just a bit late this morning. I overslept...'

'If you go on like this, you're going to be in trouble at school,' she warned him.

She's a bit behind the times, Jordan thought. 'I will be if I don't go now,' he replied.

'Listen to me, Jordan,' she said, holding onto his jacket, to make sure he was taking it in. 'You know I've never liked what she's doing any better than you, but she's so close to the end now. Please, don't go and blow it for her. Just get your act together and keep out of trouble...' *Blah...blah...blah...blah...blah...* Jordan could recite this lecture in his sleep, he'd heard it so often lately. 'Understood?' she finished.

Jordan sighed and nodded. He knew that neither she nor his uncle had wanted his mum to make this record attempt from the beginning, but by letting her do it on their land, they'd at least thought they could keep an eye on her and make sure nothing went wrong.

His aunt pulled out a handful of change. 'Now get yourself some decent lunch and call in after school and spend a bit of time with her, will you? She's really missing you.'

Jordan looked away. He pocketed the coins and, without a word, started to pedal across the gravel. Then he suddenly remembered, and turned to call back, triumphantly, 'Can't come tonight. It's Friday.'

As he rode away he said a little prayer of thanks for

Fridays. This was his night for going to his gran's for tea, the one night in the week when he could pretend his life was normal. He could enjoy his gran's cooking, get to spend time with his sister, and no one would mention his least favourite subject. Thank goodness he had that to look forward to; he'd need something to cheer him up after he'd faced Mrs Raynsworth.

By the time Jordan turned into the school gates it was gone nine. No chance now of avoiding Mrs Raynsworth's wrath. He sprinted across from the bike shed, going through his list of tried-and-tested excuses, but all of them felt stale and over-used. His teacher would have heard every one a thousand times before. How he would love to be able to surprise her: *Sorry, Miss, I was struck by lightning on my way to school; an unexploded bomb was discovered under our house; you won't believe this, Miss, but...there's an escaped man-eating tiger stalking the playground as we speak.* 'Most Far-Fetched Excuse For Late Arrival at School' was one world record Jordan would have considered worth winning. He'd happily put that in *The Gibbons Book of Weird and Wonderful World Records*. At least lying imaginatively involved some skill, not like lying down, doing nothing for five months in a coffin.

But when Jordan finally met his form teacher as she marched down the corridor with a thunderous expression on her face, he had the good sense to stick with the tried and tested. 'Sorry, Miss, I overslept...'

Mrs Raynsworth put up a hand, halting him mid-flow. 'I haven't time for your excuses, Jordan. Meet me in the detention room after school. You were warned.'

Jordan went straight to his first lesson, but arriving after it had started meant that he got his ear bent by his maths teacher too, and when he admitted he hadn't done his homework *again*, he got his second detention of the day. And it wasn't yet 9.15.

Jordan was in the top set for maths, unlike his friends, so it wasn't until swimming that he met up with them. The three of them were standing at the end of the pool, talking and flicking each other with water.

'Why don't you just get up earlier?' Anand suggested.

Jordan looked thoughtful. 'Oh, now why didn't I think of that?'

'I'm always up at six for my paper round,' Anand said, smugly.

'You're going to be on report if you keep on like this,' Martine warned Jordan. 'And stop scratching. You know you're supposed to rub if it itches.'

Jordan began to wonder how it was that he missed his mum so much when he had two friends who never stopped nagging him. He didn't look forward to swimming lessons because of his eczema, but using it as an excuse to get out of them only drew more attention to him. Guiltily Jordan stopped scratching. 'It's all right for you pair...' he started.

Anand played an air-violin while Martine told him, 'Oh, give it a rest. You've only got a couple of weeks left.'

'Yeah, you should be making the most of your last few days of freedom. I know I would be,' Anand added.

'At least you haven't got two smelly weddings to go to,' Martine pointed out.

'Uh-oh, now you've started her,' Anand complained. They'd both heard more than they wanted to already about Martine's family weddings.

Martine turned and splashed Anand full in the face, but before he could get his breath back to retaliate, their swimming teacher bellowed down the pool. 'Gibbons, Solanki, Porter – cut the chat! Five more laps!'

After the lesson, when they met up outside the changing rooms, Martine looked at Jordan for

30

a moment, smirking. 'New shirt?' she asked. 'What would you call that shade exactly? Peppermint?'

Jordan gave her a wry smile and a very rude sign.

They were suddenly overtaken by three of the boys who were generally identified as the footie crew, or as Martine liked to call them, the Dream Team: Jason Carlisle, Neil 'Nutter' Norris and Mark Ransom, aka the Biscuit, since that was all he ever ate and he had the spots to prove it.

The boys swung their bags as they passed the three friends, clipping Martine and catching Anand completely off-balance. Martine swore under her breath but wouldn't give them the satisfaction of over-reacting.

'Out the way, Skanki,' they shouted.

Anand stumbled then grinned at the boys, as if the clout had been a sign of affection and the nickname a form of endearment. 'See you later, lads,' he called after them. Jordan and Martine rolled their eyes. Anand's pathetic grovelling around the footballers made them both cringe.

'Come for a kickabout after school,' Anand suggested to Jordan. 'That'll cheer you up.'

'I've got *two* detentions, in case you've forgotten.'

'Well, after your detentions, then.'

Jordan shook his head. 'I'm not interested.'

'You used to be; you used to love it,' Anand reminded him. That's what bugged him these days: that Jordan, who was such a good player, could so easily walk away from it. To Anand, who lived for football, whose bedroom was a shrine to Leicester City Football Club, it would have been like cutting his arm off. 'You're turning into a boring old fart, you know.'

'Thanks, pal,' Jordan grinned, and used his fist to make a farting noise. Anand grinned back, pleased to see something could still make his friend smile.

Apart from double art there wasn't a lot else for Jordan to smile about for the rest of the day. His detention was even worse than he'd expected. Mrs Raynsworth gave him the longest lecture in history about being a bright boy with a good record who was throwing it all away...about how he was slipping dangerously behind and shouldn't wait till next term to pull his socks up. Unless things dramatically improved, she told him, she and all his other teachers would be forced to give him a really bad report. Had he thought how that would be for his mum? *Blah...blah...blah...blah...blah...* It felt like yet more emotional blackmail.

Jordan went silent and tuned out, but Mrs Raynsworth wasn't letting him off that easily. She seemed determined to save Jordan from himself. 'I've seen other good pupils, just like you, throw it all away,' she told him. 'Believe me, Jordan, a good reputation is far harder to get back than it is to lose.'

When it was finally over, Jordan heaved a thankful sigh. But his relief was short-lived when he was ambushed by Mr Hart, along with two other boys who had detentions, and roped in for one of the head teacher's infamous litter picks.

By the time Jordan left it was properly dark, and he had to cycle on the pavements because his lights weren't working. Halfway home he remembered that Jet had been in on his own all day after failing to perform that morning. Jordan pedalled as hard as he could, hoping to get back before anyone else, in case there had been any accidents. But as he rode up his street, he could see lights already on in the house.

In the kitchen his brother, Kyle, was cleaning his boots, getting ready for the TA that evening. 'You, little brother,' he told Jordan, with a grin on his face, 'are in deep doggy-do.' He pointed the shoe brush towards the lounge. '*Literally.*'

When Jordan went through he found a large unsavoury pile still steaming on the carpet and a very guilty-looking dog peeping out from behind the sofa. How could his brother have just left it there?

'Why didn't you clear it up?' Jordan yelled through to Kyle.

'Not my dog,' came the reply.

CHAPTER THREE

Jordan carried the offending pile through the kitchen in a bunch of kitchen towel and dumped it in the wheelie bin outside. He found the carpet spray and squirted the whole area. He'd done this job enough times lately to be quite expert at it. He could see Jet watching him, still half-hidden behind the sofa. Jordan wanted to be cross with him, but it wasn't the dog's fault; it was his brother that Jordan was furious with. How could he have just left it there, smelling the place out?

Kyle, still polishing his boots, stood in the doorway watching him.

'You could have cleared it up,' Jordan told him again.

'You could have made sure the doors were closed,' Kyle argued.

'I *did*!' Jordan insisted; he clearly remembered doing it. But then he'd come back in for his swimming gear, hadn't he?

'How come you're so late home, anyway?'

'Detention,' Jordan admitted.

'Why can't you just stay out of trouble?' Kyle asked. 'It's not like you're expected to do anything else.'

Jordan kept his head down. The last thing he wanted was another argument with Kyle. What was the point, they would never agree on this one...

Jordan wished he could be more like his brother and get completely behind his mum. Every evening and weekend his dad and Kyle took it in turns to be up there at the burial site, keeping her company, lifting her spirits whenever they flagged, encouraging her to do her exercises, monitoring her health. She was the one under the ground, actually trying to achieve the world record, but their lives were equally focused on it – and they didn't resent it, not for a minute.

And his brother still found time to train for his own record attempt, too: Kyle and a friend were planning a three-legged marathon, from Land's End to John o' Groats. Yet another totally pointless exercise in Jordan's eyes, although not quite as pointless as lying lifeless in a box, he thought.

'That sounds like Dad's car now,' Kyle announced. 'You'd better get a move on.'

Jordan gave the carpet a final blast of cleaner then blotted it as dry as he could. That would have to do, even though it still smelled rank. Then he quickly put Jet on his lead, ready to make his getaway as his dad opened the door. They just avoided actually colliding.

'Steady! It's a bit late for a dog walk, isn't it?' his dad asked.

'I'm off to Gran's,' Jordan reminded him. 'It's Friday?'

'Well, give us a hug first,' he said.

Jordan leaned briefly against his dad in the doorway and allowed himself to be hugged. At thirteen he thought he was too old for that kind of thing, although the truth was he missed it more than he cared to admit.

'Shall I collect you on my way home?' his dad asked.

'No, thanks,' Jordan called from halfway down the path. He'd safely reached the gate before he heard his dad's voice suddenly rising. *'God, what is that smell?!'*

*

Jordan's gran lived several streets away. He could have found his way there blindfolded. When he was little, and his mum had gone back to work, he'd almost lived at his grandparents' house. Until his grandpa had died two years ago, he'd spent whole days with him fishing on the river, or on Rutland Water, or in Derbyshire.

Jordan sighed as he thought about how much had changed since then. Now he saw his gran a measly once a week. He could have gone there more often, he knew that. He could have moved in with her, like his sister had – but that would have been disloyal to his mum. It would have been like admitting that his dad couldn't cope; that Jordan was really missing out, because of what his mum was doing. Couldn't let people think that! Once-a-week visits were OK and kept everyone happy – everyone except Jordan.

He let himself in the back door and felt as if he'd walked into an advert. The wonderful cooking smells made him realise how hungry he was. He tried to guess: probably one of his gran's stews – with dumplings – maybe an apple pie or a sticky pudding with custard.

Jordan's mum used to make meals like this, before she got into all this world-record nonsense. When he was younger, and he and Kyle had swimming lessons, they'd regularly come home to some hot steaming casserole and a big fruit crumble. Sometimes they'd eat so much they couldn't get up from the table, and their dad had christened it *fruit stumble*.

Jordan's dad had never done any cooking himself, and he really didn't have time to learn now. It was always instant food, often not properly cooked through, so the outside burnt your tongue while the middle was still frozen. It was only recently that Jordan had come to realise quite how much he loved food. Even though he was probably getting *enough* to eat, these days he seemed to feel permanently hungry.

'You're late, lad. Where've you been till now?' his gran asked, giving Jordan a peck on the cheek. 'Oh, I see you've brought a friend along. Make sure he wipes his feet.'

She threw an old towel to Jordan, who gave his own feet an extra rub on the mat, then knelt to wipe Jet's paws. He omitted to mention the detention and blamed being late on the dog. 'When I got home from school he'd done a pile on the carpet and I had to clear it up before Dad came in. It smelled vile.'

'Too much information,' his sister called from the sitting room.

'He'd better not do that here,' his gran warned.

Jordan kept Jet on a very short lead until he'd calmed down. His gran loved dogs, but not badly behaved ones.

'I can't imagine what your father was thinking,' she said, not for the first time, 'getting a dog like this.' Jet was a border collie, a breed that needed masses of exercise and proper training, and a boy of thirteen could hardly be responsible for that in her view. 'Guilt makes people do some very silly things,' she added cryptically.

But she soon softened and couldn't resist giving Jet a bit of a fuss and a couple of treats. Jordan left them in the kitchen and went through to the sitting room, where his sister, Chrissie, was half-watching *The Simpsons* on TV.

'So, how's life at the madhouse?' she asked.

'Mad as ever,' Jordan told her.

'How's Dad?'

'OK.'

She patted the space beside her on the sofa. 'Come and give us a cuddle,' she ordered. Jordan groaned and pretended to push her away, but he wasn't fooling anyone, and when she started to wrestle with him he soon conceded. Sitting cosily, leaning against his sister in front of the TV, was just one of the many things Jordan missed nowadays. He didn't even mind when she flattened his carefully gelled hair – although he pushed it back into shape at the first opportunity.

Chrissie was eighteen and worked in a bank. She had a boyfriend, confusingly called Chris, who worked in the same bank. They were saving up for their first holiday together and Chrissie was poring over brochures.

'Where you going?' Jordan asked.

'Dunno, somewhere hot and sunny. I'm thinking Lanzarote.'

'You lucky devil.'

'Luck has nothing to do with it,' Chrissie insisted. 'I've worked hard for this.'

'Food's ready,' their gran called, and they got up and made a race for the table, almost upending a chair in the process, just as if they were both about seven years old.

'You'd think neither of you had eaten in a week,' his gran laughed, then looked at Jordan. 'And you look like it, an' all.'

She was always commenting on how thin he was looking these days, so Jordan had to pretend he ate like this every day. He loved coming here, but could never completely relax, because if he gave either his gran or his sister the slightest opening they'd start criticising his mum and he'd be forced to defend her, even though he didn't *want* to defend her – he mostly agreed with them.

As much as he tried, it wasn't easy avoiding the big subject. There was so little else at the moment that Jordan *could* talk about; he couldn't talk about his detentions and his troubles at school, or his friend, Anand, nicking from his dad's shop. In the end it oftencame back to his mum, and despite his best efforts Jordan found himself saying, 'Only eighteen days to go.'

'Thank God for that,' said his gran. 'I pray I never have to live through it another time. I think it'd kill me.'

Jordan might not like what his mum was doing, but it seemed even worse for his gran. She was so upset – and embarrassed – about it that she'd stopped going to bingo or down to the Social Club at the weekend. Chrissie did all her shopping for her now; she'd pretty well turned into a hermit, just to avoid seeing people in case anyone brought up the subject.

When his mum had first decided on her record attempt there had been an awful row; Jordan had been there.

'You know how much I hated it the first time round, when your dad did it,' his gran had said. 'I can't believe you're expecting me to do it all over again.'

'You're not the one who's going to be doing it,' his mum had laughed.

But that had just made his gran angrier. 'It's not much more than a year since I lost your father and now you expect me to watch my own daughter being buried?'

'It's hardly the same,' his mum had tried to reason with her.

'It's an insult to God, Debbie, that's what it is,' his gran had shouted. 'It's like saying your life's worthless, means nothing.'

This had seemed so over-the-top to Jordan's mum that she'd laughed again. 'Come on, Mum,' she'd said, trying to calm his gran down. 'We're only talking five months.'

'A lot of things can happen in five months,' Gran had said darkly.

Jordan's gran was only in her mid-sixties but she already saw herself as an old person, and having lost her husband, was already hinting she might not have many years left herself. Whenever you made any future plans with his gran, she always added, 'God willing'.

His mum said it was all nonsense, that his gran was

43

as fit as a flea and would probably outlive them all, but she wouldn't be placated.

'She'll come round,' his mum had insisted. 'She just likes a bit of a moan.'

But his gran hadn't come round. She'd refused to even talk about it again and his mum had been buried without them making up their quarrel.

His sister, Chrissie, had taken their gran's side from the outset. 'Gran's right, it's a pathetic idea,' she told her mum. 'How will I face my friends? I shall *die* of embarrassment.'

'Not very likely,' her mum had said, smiling.

'But what will people think?' Chrissie cried, her head in her hands.

'You shouldn't care so much what other people think,' her mum told her.

'If you didn't care what other people thought, why else would you be doing it?' Chrissie had demanded.

To Jordan's mind his mum hadn't been able to give a satisfactory answer to that.

'Well, don't expect me to come and visit *your grave*,' his sister had said bitterly, and the next day she'd moved out. She'd gone to live at their gran's, splitting the family in two, leaving Jordan in some sort of no-man's-land in the middle.

Jordan wished yet again that his grandpa were still alive. If he were, he'd have asked him what it had been like for him, when he did it. And what had made him do it in the first place. He asked his gran now instead, and she reluctantly told him.

'He always said he'd led such a boring life, that he'd never done anything out of the ordinary. He suddenly got it into his head that he wanted a world record. It didn't really matter to him what it was. He just got obsessed with it.'

'But why that particular record?' Jordan pressed her.

'Well,' his gran smiled, 'every day he came home from work, ate his dinner and fell asleep in the chair, as regular as clockwork. Apart from fishing, that was his life. So when he was trying to think of something he might have a talent for, like a fool, I said, "You know what you're good at – sleeping." And that was it.'

Jordan smiled. He remembered how his grandpa could fall asleep in a second, on a hard kitchen chair, on the back step, where he went to have a quiet cigarette, on the riverbank, sitting on his fishing box...and probably, as his gran used to joke, on a clothesline, if he'd really set his mind to it.

'After all, he'd worked down the mines since he was

a boy,' his gran went on, 'so he wasn't afraid of the dark, or small spaces.' She sighed. 'I blame myself – if I hadn't given him the idea, he might never have done it.'

'He'd have probably done something equally silly, Gran,' Chrissie told her. 'You know how stubborn he could be.'

'Didn't you all miss him?' Jordan asked.

'Of course we missed him,' his gran replied. 'But don't forget, your mum and your uncle were much younger than you are. Matthew was seven and your mum was only five. They were on the pleasure beach all day long. It was one big holiday for them.'

When his grandpa set the record, he'd been buried on the East Coast, beside an amusement park close to the sea front. The family had stayed over there, living in a hotel the whole time so they could be with him. Jordan's mum always said she had nothing but happy memories of the time. Perhaps he'd have been able to enjoy it more if he'd been a little kid on holiday – instead of having to go to school every day, getting detentions, then coming home to an empty house and his dad's kitchen disasters.

Jordan couldn't understand why he'd known so little about his grandpa's record while he was still alive. It was hardly ever mentioned in the family. It was only when his grandpa died and the local paper rang his mum and asked her about the record that everyone started talking about it. The reporter had wanted to know if anyone else in the family was going to try to get the record back from the American for her dad.

'Don't be so daft,' she'd told him. It hadn't been long after Grandpa had died and at first she'd been upset and cross with the reporter. But after she put down the phone the idea seemed to have lodged itself in her brain. Soon she'd convinced herself.

'It'd be like a tribute to your grandpa,' she'd told Jordan. 'Can you understand that?'

But Jordan hadn't understood. And later, when his dad had tried to explain – 'I think she's really missing him, you know' – Jordan had thought, *big deal!* He missed his grandpa too. He'd been the one who'd spent the most time with him. He desperately missed their fishing trips.

At least Jordan could console himself with the thought that tomorrow was Saturday and he was free to go fishing. Not with his grandpa, but on his own, which wasn't quite the same.

Thank goodness he had the dog for company now.

Jet was the most sympathetic ear he had to pour out his troubles to these days. Jordan stood under a lamppost while he waited patiently for the dog to finish his investigations.

'I hope the lounge smells a bit better by the time we get home,' Jordan told Jet. With a bit of luck he'd be in bed before his dad came in to tell him off about the mess on the carpet. 'We're going to have to be a bit more careful,' he warned. 'No more accidents, OK?'

But the dog was far too engrossed in the subtle scents of the lamppost to bother with a reply.

CHAPTER FOUR

Jordan's fishing box was packed and waiting near the door by 7.30 the next morning, when Kyle came in from his training run. Kyle, who was pink and very sweaty, didn't see the box and almost tripped over it, which didn't improve his temper. Jordan was in the kitchen preparing a flask of chicken soup and some Marmite sandwiches to take with him.

'For goodness' sake,' Kyle complained, but he flipped the box lid open and grudgingly admired the neatly organised tackle. He wondered aloud, 'Can this be the same person whose bedroom would put the average pig to shame?'

Jordan kept his head down. He didn't want to get

into an argument this morning. He was in a good mood and wanted to stay that way.

'And can this person, who has no trouble getting up at the crack of dawn for fishing, be the same someone who can't get to school on time any day of the week?'

Jordan shrugged. It was a fair question and he didn't have a good answer.

'I hope for your sake that's not the last of the bread you're using,' Kyle warned him.

Jordan held up a couple of crusts he'd thoughtfully left for his brother's breakfast.

'Well, you can add an extra loaf to the list Dad's left. I'm going up for a shower, just make sure it's here for when I get down.'

'Aww, man, I'm about to go fishing.'

'Not till those jobs are done, you're not.'

Kyle pointed to the fridge. Jordan's dad was a self-employed electrician. He worked long hours and was already at work most days before Jordan got up, including Saturdays. He often left messages for him, sometimes a list of jobs too, stuck by a magnet to the fridge door. Jordan had seen the list, which told him to change his sheets – a job he'd been ignoring for over a week already; bring down his dirty washing – ditto; do some shopping; plus the strict instruction, heavily underlined, to go and visit his mum that morning.

'I'll do them all this afternoon,' he promised.

'You'll do them this morning,' Kyle insisted.

'It's not fair,' Jordan almost whined. He could hear himself sounding about six years old.

Kyle's face confirmed it. 'When are you going to grow up? Why can't you consider Mum for a change? She wants to see you, God only knows why.'

Jordan couldn't provide an excuse; he simply didn't want to go up there, and his face gave him away.

'Oh, for goodness' sake, get off fishing,' Kyle growled. 'I'll do the shopping on my way to the farm. But make sure you get your other jobs done later. And if you don't go up to see Mum *this afternoon* you'll have me to answer to, understood?'

'Thanks,' Jordan smiled, winningly.

Kyle didn't return the smile. He wanted his brother to know that he, for one, was immune to the famous smile. Jordan had that fair hair, blue eyes and soft tanned skin that many girls admire, plus the killer smile. Until more recently, when he'd started to mess up, this smile had always been Jordan's secret weapon. It had kept him in everyone's good books. Whenever he flashed it, his mum and dad, his sister, his gran, his teachers, most of the other kids at school – especially the girls – couldn't seem to stay mad with him for long. Only Kyle was unimpressed – and Martine. If ever Jordan tried it on her she narrowed her eyes and told him, 'Don't waste your energy, Gibbons. I can see right through you.'

Martine wasn't like most other girls in their class; she wasn't a tomboy, exactly, she was just...different. She had a very sharp tongue that she often used to keep him and Anand firmly in their places. As far as Martine was concerned, the two boys needed her guiding influence, and she often wondered aloud where on earth they would end up without it.

Jordan promised himself he would turn over a new leaf; that when he got home from fishing he'd do all his jobs *and* he'd visit his mum. But for now all he could think about was getting out, on his own, down the river.

He couldn't understand why time spent alone at home often made him feel lonely, and yet being on his own by the river for hours never had that effect.

'There's no comparison,' his grandpa told him. 'This is called *solitude*. Most people don't understand the difference.'

Although they would sit fairly close to one another while they fished, they rarely talked, sometimes staying silent for hours at a time. Jordan had found it hard when he was younger, but he'd gradually learned to concentrate his attention on the river, to notice the tiny signs that might hint there were fish below the surface.

'It might seem as if there's not much happening,' his grandpa always said, 'but the river's constantly moving, constantly changing – a seething world of wildlife, if you keep your eyes open to it.'

Jordan set off on his bike now, his fishing box on a long strap across his back, his rods tied to his crossbar. It was still early and there was frost on the trees and the cars as he rode along the road. He had three layers beneath his waterproof, which had been his grandpa's and was a bit big for him, but not a lot. He would have to grow into his grandpa's boots, though, still a good two sizes too big. The fishing box he'd inherited, too, in fact all his gear: his rods and reels, his floats, his flies, even his place on the river had now come to Jordan.

He loved the fact that the regular fishermen who'd known his grandpa had all assumed the spot would now be Jordan's. Down the river, at least, he was one of the men – unlike at home, where he was still treated as the baby of the family.

Along the towpath he stopped briefly by his grandpa's bench. It bore a little plaque that read:

In Memory of Billy Craig
1936–2006
Gone Fishing – Won't Be Back

His grandpa had chosen the words himself and told Jordan what the plaque should say. Not that he was expecting to die any time soon. He'd been in good health, as far as everyone knew. He'd simply died of a heart attack by the river, while he was fishing on his own on a weekday.

Jordan used his sleeve to polish up the little plaque. Even though the doctor had told them his grandpa had died outright, that nothing could have been done for him, Jordan still couldn't let go of the idea that had he been with him at the time he could have saved him, or at least called an ambulance, got some help.

His grandpa had fallen forward out of his seat and partly slipped into the river. It was a dog-walker who'd found him and called the police. Jordan thought how cross his grandpa would have been to have broken his record, because he liked to brag that he had never in all his years of fishing ever fallen into the water.

Jordan cycled on until he came in sight of his fishing spot. His grandpa had been fishing for a lifetime and it was a well-chosen swim. It was in the margins, far enough away from the path not to be disturbed by cyclists and dog walkers. It had enough structure – large overhanging trees and reeds – to provide shelter for the fish from the heat of the summer sun. The river was deep enough at this point for fish to have somewhere to hide, and at the wide bend the current provided an additional challenge for the fisherman.

Jordan laid his bike where he could keep his eye on it and unloaded his gear: his keep net, his landing net, his bait boxes and two rods. He selected the lighter rod, putting it together and choosing a four-pound line which would take the weight of a perch or chubb or even a good-sized carp: all fish he knew he might possibly catch here.

He chose his bait carefully, following his grandpa's instructions: 'No sense offering hemp to a big-mouthed fish, like bream,' he'd told Jordan, 'and no self-respecting carp's going to be tempted by a measly maggot. It's horses for courses.'

Today Jordan was after perch or roach. He opened his tub of worms and lifted one out, slicing it neatly in half. These were not just any old garden worms; they were *dendrebena*, European woodland worms. His grandpa swore by them and bought them from a local tackle shop.

Jordan attached his bait then added a float to warn him when a fish was biting. He chose a waggler, which made it possible to cast a longer distance with greater accuracy, helping him get the bait to where the fish were and keep it there.

Before he sank his line he baited up the whole area. His grandpa liked to use a baiting cup attached to the end of his rod, but Jordan had his own method – a catapult. He loaded it with a handful of chopped worms then fired it expertly to hit the spot he'd chosen. Then he stood on the bank and cast his line, nice and smooth, letting his rod do the work for him. He gave a couple of sharp turns on his reel while jerking the rod to one side to make sure his line was fully submerged. At this time of year, with little leaf cover overhead, the fish would see a line left sitting on the surface. When he was perfectly satisfied, Jordan sat back on his box and waited.

His mobile began to ring. He ignored it, and after a couple of seconds it vibrated in his pocket, telling him a text had come in. But he took out his phone and, without even bothering to look, turned it off. He didn't want to be disturbed this morning by anyone.

Whenever he was fishing it was hard for Jordan not to think about his grandpa. He still quite often turned to speak to him before he remembered. Jordan had cried more than he'd cried in his entire life when his grandpa died. He'd cried when he first heard the news, he'd cried every night in bed for a week, and he'd cried again at the funeral. But Jordan hadn't cried like his mum had, sobbing, gulping almost. He'd hated seeing her like that. Even his gran had held it together better. She'd been annoyed with his mum; he'd heard her say she should pull herself together.

Looking back, Jordan could see that his mum hadn't really been quite herself ever since. She hadn't had as much life in her, hadn't been interested in anything – not until she'd had this idea of winning back her dad's world record.

Jordan saw the waggler quivering before he felt a tiny movement in his line. He could tell it was nothing to get excited about, maybe some tiddly little roach or even a gudgeon. It didn't put up much of a fight and he easily pulled in his line and carefully extracted the hook from the tiny fish's mouth. Kneeling down, he fed it quickly back into the water, watching it disappear in a nanosecond.

Jordan rebaited his line and recast it, then he sat back and waited again.

There were only one or two other fishermen in sight: his grandpa's mate, Stanley, and another man Jordan only knew by sight. Only hardy anglers came out in December to brave the cold and the rain. In summer all the fair-weather fishermen appeared – like bugs crawling out of the woodwork, his grandpa used to say, grumpily.

It made no difference to Jordan whatever the weather or time of year. He was in love with the very business of fishing and it didn't even matter whether he caught anything or not. There was always something different to see. In winter, when the leaves were off the trees, you could see birds that in summer would have been hidden. And he liked to watch the ever-moving river and imagine what might suddenly emerge from it, what excitement it promised, what life-and-death struggles.

He had once tried to initiate his friends into this private world of his, but they were never impressed. It was far too slow for Anand, who needed something more active to hold his interest. Anand's own obsession with football caused everything else to pale into insignificance.

For Martine, fishing went against all her moral principles. As she once told Jordan, 'Quite frankly, I think it's barbaric! If I was prime minister I'd ban it.'

Martine would watch any animal rescue programme on TV and spill real tears over virtually every animal that appeared on it. It was one of her many grudges against her parents that she was not allowed a single pet of her own.

'When I grow up I shall be one of those weird old women who feeds all the strays. I shall have as many animals as I want. I shall have a flaming zoo if I feel like it,' she sometimes declared.

Jordan sighed and relaxed fully for the first time in a week. When he was by the river, during these long stretches on his own, he could think, or choose not to think – especially about his mum. He leaned back, anticipating a long peaceful morning entirely to himself.

He'd had less than an hour to enjoy the solitude when he suddenly heard his name yelled at full volume all the way down the riverbank. 'Hey, Gibbo! Look who's come to see you!'

CHAPTER FIVE

Jordan didn't like to admit it, even to himself, but the sight of Anand and Martine – his absolutely best mates – walking towards him, made his heart sink. He was embarrassed by the noise they were making; he could see the other fishermen further down the bank giving them dirty looks.

'Keep it down, can't you?' he told them when they finally reached him. 'People are trying to fish here.'

'God, man, you sound like my nani ma: *people are trying to sleep here...*' Anand said in his grandmother's complaining voice.

'We thought we'd come and cheer you up,' Martine said, plopping herself down on the grass beside him.

'It'll be wet,' he warned.

'Shift your bony bottom then,' she said, squeezing beside him on his fishing box instead.

'We've been calling you and calling you,' Anand grumbled, 'but your phone was off.'

'Yeah, well…now you sound like my gran.'

'Can I have a go with this one?' Anand asked, reaching for Jordan's spare rod.

'Here, hold this,' Jordan told Martine as he passed her his rod, then set about preparing and casting the second line before handing it to Anand. Then he stood around while his two friends sat side by side on his box.

'Now what?' Anand asked.

'Now you wait,' Jordan told him. 'And you try to be quiet. Otherwise you'll frighten the fish away.'

'Yeah, one look at your ugly mug and they'll be off,' Martine told Anand.

It wasn't long before Anand was sighing heavily. 'I don't get it. Where's the action, man, where's the buzz?'

Jordan had never really been able to explain the thrill of fishing because it wasn't instant, like some sports, but he tried his best.

'The waiting's all part of it. It's called *anticipation*.

You've got to expect quiet times, but then, when you get a bite, especially if it's a decent-sized fish that's determined to fight back...it's just the best feeling.' That was the action; that was the buzz, for Jordan anyway; but he could see by his friends' faces that they were still unconvinced. 'Anyway, you've only been here two minutes. Show a bit of patience,' he told them, grumpily.

'You've got to admit, though, it's not like footie,' Anand argued.

Jordan shrugged. 'You can't compare them.'

'You can,' Martine muttered. 'They're both boring with a capital "B".'

Anand ignored Martine and agreed with Jordan. 'You certainly can't compare them. For a start, fishing's an old man's game, and for another, you'd earn far more as a footballer than you ever would as a fisherman. When I play for Leicester City I shall probably earn...half a million...'

'In your dreams,' Martine cut him off.

Everyone knew that Anand's passion for the game sadly outstripped his talent. Jordan, on the other hand, could have been a really good player – one of the best. The football crew had been onto Anand to get Jordan back into the game for some time, and recently they'd made it a condition of letting Anand play. He was running out of time and arguments to convince his friend.

Already bored, Anand passed his fishing rod back to Jordan. He reached in his pocket for some sweetener he could offer Jordan and held out a Snickers bar. But before his friend could take it, he snatched it back. 'Hang on,' he said, smiling, 'there's a price: you have to play footie this afternoon.'

But Jordan shook his head. 'Can't, gotta see my mum. And even if I could...don't want to. Sorry.' Anand sighed and offered the chocolate bar to Martine instead.

She looked at it longingly and was about to take it when Jordan reminded her, 'Think of the weddings.'

Martine quietly seethed. 'I hate my family,' she said with feeling. With two weddings coming soon her mum and sister had turned into the food police.

'Can you believe there's a lock on the fridge now?' she complained. 'Stu lost his temper the other day when my mum was out. He couldn't even make a cup of tea cos the milk was in the fridge and she'd taken the key with her. They had a filthy row and the wedding was off.'

'That's good news, isn't it?' Anand congratulated her. They all knew that Stu, her mum's boyfriend, was Martine's least favourite person in the world.

But Martine only shrugged. 'It was back on the next day.'

'Well, it'll all soon be over,' Jordan said, trying to cheer her up.

'That's rich coming from you, who can't wait, what is it now, eighteen days?'

'Seventeen, actually,' Jordan corrected her.

'At least when your mum comes out things'll get back to normal for you. You won't have to live the rest of your life with the family from the funny farm.'

This was a frequently rehearsed argument. Competing with one another over who had the weirdest family was the nearest thing the three friends had to a shared hobby. In Jordan's view, his mum's decision to be buried alive for nearly five months made him far and away the winner. How could either of his two friends ever top that? But Martine held her family up against all-comers.

'At least you're not expected to be a bridesmaid at *two* different weddings on the *same* day,' she declared. 'It's like they're competing to see who can have the most embarrassing wedding in the world.' Both her mother *and* her sister were having themed weddings: her mum's country and western, her sister's based on the film *Titanic*. 'It's pathetic,' she snarled. 'I can't decide which'll be worse, watching my sister pretend to be Kate Winslet, or seeing my mum break out in cowboy boots and a mini skirt, but you can bet it'll be a close thing.'

Martine was nowhere near obese, but at thirteen she was still carrying what she fervently hoped would still prove to be puppy fat. So the final straw for her was that she was being forced to squeeze herself into two disgusting dresses, both of which were designed to make her the laughing stock of the century.

Anand looked a bit bored with the whole subject. He'd told Jordan privately that it certainly didn't look like this diet was working and Martine should jack it in. Jordan, on the other hand, had tried to be supportive, giving her encouragement every time she felt the chocolate rush, but he was beginning to agree with Anand. The evidence was clear. The longer Martine had been on a diet, the bigger she seemed to be getting. She'd gone from a bit round at the edges to bordering on fat, but Jordan had the sense to keep this opinion to himself.

'Well, d'you want it, or not?' Anand was still

waving the chocolate bar in her direction and Martine was still wavering.

Jordan offered her his chicken soup as an alternative, but Martine looked as if he'd offered her a flask of rat poison. 'I don't think so.'

The subject of weight was an increasingly sore one for Martine. Because of the weddings they now had family membership of Weight Watchers, and she was dragged there weekly to experience the humiliation of a public weighing. And yet her weight had steadily risen and both bridesmaid dresses had had to be let out twice already, a fact which gave her some small satisfaction.

'Anyway, you haven't heard the latest,' she told the others, glad to be off the subject of food. 'Guess who's giving them both away?'

The boys shrugged and waited for the revelation.

'*My dad!*' she announced with glee.

The boys proved a disappointing audience.

'That's good, isn't it?' Anand shrugged.

'It means your mum and dad are still friends,' Jordan agreed.

'*Noooo!*' Martine almost yelled at them. 'It means he's as barmy as she is, which means I get a double helping of the crazy genes! Madhouse, here I come!'

Jordan grinned. Whenever Martine got this worked up she always made him laugh. He knew this wasn't the reaction she was looking for, but he couldn't honestly take it seriously. How could she possibly compare all her family's admittedly embarrassing behaviour with the *world-class weirdness* of his situation?

Lately, even Anand seemed determined to join the contest, despite the other two telling him it was a no-brainer. He'd been giving them updates on what he called his own dad's creeping craziness.

Anand's dad was not only deeply pessimistic by nature, he was also blindly superstitious – in Anand's view. He could see bad omens in almost anything that happened directly to him, as well as in any general piece of bad news, of which the newspapers were filled daily. According to Anand his dad positively relished disasters, natural or otherwise. And yet the more distressed his father became the more it seemed to amuse Anand.

'This is not so funny a joking matter,' his dad frequently told him, and Anand now repeated to his friends. ' "*For your information – which is a thing that is poorly lacking – the world is heading headlong for disaster.*" '

Now, with the escalating cost of fuel and talk of recession, Anand's father had convinced himself that the whole country and all its public services would soon break down into chaos, and even food would soon be in short supply.

'So now he's started stockpiling tins under everyone's beds,' Anand announced. 'He says that when shops start to run out at least we won't be hungry. "*I do not think you realise, my boy, that the world – as we know it – may be on the brinking of disaster,*"' Anand mimicked. 'So I said, if that's the case, Pop, can I have next month's pocket money in advance?'

'What did he say?' Jordan asked.

'He gave me a clip round the ear.'

Martine suddenly sat up, squealing, 'Something's happening.' She panicked and pushed the rod towards Anand, since Jordan was already holding one.

The whole rod was bending under the weight of the catch and Anand struggled to get a grip on it. 'Hey, this is quite exciting, innit?' he said, grinning. Martine, despite herself, was hopping about too.

'Shh,' Jordan hushed them. 'Hold it steady! Now reel it in, not too much... Wait! No, that's too much. Let it out again. Wait... Now reel it in again...'

He kept up careful instructions, encouraging Anand to alternate between giving the fish some extra line and then pulling it back. They repeated this process for what seemed to Anand an absolute age.

'My arms are aching,' he moaned. 'Can't we hurry up?'

Jordan ignored him and continued his instructions until a big silver chubb briefly broke the surface. It dropped back into the water but only a short way, so they could see it clearly now. He ordered Anand to hold the line steady, while he used the landing net to scoop the fish up.

Anand was puffing and panting as if he'd run a race.

'Call yourself fit,' Martine mocked. 'So much for your precious football career.'

'It's hard work,' Anand conceded. 'My arms are about dropping off.' But he was beaming as if the catch had been his own work entirely.

The other two watched as Jordan crouched down and drew the line towards him, finally cradling the fish in his hands. It was big enough to impress them and they both leaned forward for a closer look. It wasn't a pretty fish, with its big wide mouth, but it touched Martine's heart.

'Oh, the poor thing,' she whimpered.

'It's quite big, innit?' Anand remarked, touching the fish with a finger. 'Feels slimy, though,' he said, pulling a face.

Jordan carefully retrieved the hook from the fish's mouth and then knelt on the bank, holding the chubb for a moment half underwater to let his friends get another look before releasing it and watching it dart away.

'Why d'you do that?' Anand said, astonished.

'You always put the fish back,' Jordan said simply.

'You catch them just for the fun of it?' Martine said. 'That's even worse.'

'If you're not going to eat it,' Anand agreed, 'what's the point?'

Jordan just shrugged. 'It's a sport.'

'Sport?!' Martine exploded. 'It's cruelty, that's what it is. You're not telling me that hook doesn't hurt its mouth.'

Jordan gave up the argument. He didn't believe that it hurt the fish, but he couldn't prove otherwise. How could he begin to explain to his friends the thrill of freeing a fish, the sensation of it darting from his hand, the feel of it even for a second resting in his palm, gently pulsating, before slipping away into the undergrowth. No point even trying.

'So, that's it?' Anand asked. 'That's all we were waiting for?'

Jordan smiled at the question. He shook his head and then started to set up his line again.

'I can see why girls don't fish,' Martine said.

'Some girls do,' Jordan told her. 'It was a girl set the record for the largest salmon ever caught. It weighed *sixty-four pounds*!'

'No kidding,' Martine said, unimpressed.

'It was in Scotland: the heaviest freshwater fish ever caught in British waters – and that was by a girl.'

'Now you're boring me,' she said. 'Anyway, gotta go.' She curled her lip. 'Another smelly dress fitting. With a bit of luck they'll have to let it out again. See you later,' she called.

'Not if we see you first,' the two boys chorused.

Martine turned and gave them a weary look before walking slowly down the towpath.

The two boys sat side by side in companionable silence for a while, until Anand once more inevitably started to get fidgety. He sighed a lot and was soon throwing twigs into the water, making quite sure Jordan was never going to catch anything. When he could see that his friend wasn't about to go away and leave him in peace, Jordan started to pack up his gear and the two of them walked home together, Anand pushing Jordan's bike.

'Are you absolutely sure you won't come down this afternoon?' Anand asked again, more than a hint of pleading in his voice.

'I've gotta see my mum, I promised.'

'They won't let me play any more,' Anand admitted, 'unless you come.'

Jordan groaned. He wanted to contradict his friend, but he knew the football crew only too well.

There used to be a time when no one ran the game; whoever brought the ball chose the teams and what few rules they had were generally agreed and kept to. But this year a couple of older boys had taken over: one called Connor who'd recently moved down from Scotland and was known as Scotty-boy, and another he'd palled up with, Ricky Doherty, who'd always liked to think of himself as a hard character, and now had someone even harder to back him up.

The two boys ran the football game a bit like a small-scale mafia racket. Ricky Doherty had a range of threats he used: *I'll mark him, I'll bang him out, I'll take his leg out.* And Connor Stewart had added a few of his own, which had a hospital theme: *I'll leave him lying in a hospital bed.* Behind their backs the two boys were nicknamed Hit and Run – they made a formidable pair.

They had collected a gang around them that included the three boys from Jordan's class who Anand was always trying to get in with: Jason Carlisle, also famous for his fouling, Nutter Norris and the Biscuit.

Nowadays there were only two ways to get into the football game. You either had to be really good at football – which Anand wasn't – or you had to have something the boys wanted. Robby Irwin, for instance, wasn't the best player on the planet, but he sometimes did their maths homework for them. Anand had been allowed in, under sufferance, as Jordan's friend.

'I haven't been playing for months,' Jordan pointed out. 'And they've still let you play.'

'Only because I've managed to keep them sweet,' Anand admitted, patting his pocket. 'Who do you think the ciggies are for?'

'You're an idiot,' Jordan told his friend. 'How long did you think you could keep that up?'

'For ever, when it was just sweets, but my dad's already started missing the ciggies.'

'Aw, man, what are you going to do?'

Anand shrugged. 'Emigrate?'

The two boys separated at the end of Anand's street and Jordan continued to push his bike, balancing his fishing box on the cross bar. He was concerned about his friend and felt partly responsible. He could have gone down with Anand from time to time for a kickabout, just to keep the other boys happy. He knew he was being selfish, but Jordan couldn't stand the football crowd any more. They always made stupid, inane jokes about his mum that drove him mad.

Connor Stewart, when he first heard about Jordan's mum, had asked if she was some kind of psycho. 'Must run in the family,' he told Jordan.

But if he was being totally honest, Jordan had to admit that he just couldn't make the effort. These days, apart from fishing, he simply couldn't be bothered with anything any more.

As they parted, Jordan had told Anand to keep away from the boys for a while. 'Just don't give them any more stuff. They can't make you.'

But Anand gave him a look that let Jordan know his

friend's advice was not what he was looking for – and he clearly wouldn't be taking it.

In the past Anand would have listened to him, because Jordan would have had real answers to offer, real ideas to fix the situation. But he wasn't *the Fixer* any more. He felt as if his influence over his friend had completely slipped away and he wasn't sure how that had happened.

CHAPTER SIX

It was late Sunday morning and Jordan, still in his pyjamas, was lying on the sofa. He was home alone, although he needn't have been. He could have gone up to the farm with his dad and his brother, but Jordan had used homework, and the fact that he still had his bed to change and his clothes to sort out, as an excuse not to go. He promised he'd go up later, but even as he said it Jordan knew he wouldn't go, and probably wouldn't do any of those jobs either.

Sunday was Jordan's worst day of the week. Staying at home on his own meant he was almost certain to be bored – out of his skull – almost to screaming point. His friends were usually busy: Anand often had to work in the shop, or, like today, his family had relatives visiting; Martine usually spent the day with her dad. Walking the dog or fishing could fill a few hours on a dry day, but right now it was pouring with rain, so neither was an option.

On the other hand, Sundays up at the farm were the absolute pits. There was no point trying to talk to his mum, because he'd never get near her. Visiting *the woman in a box* had become a popular local day out. The café did a roaring trade in Sunday roast dinners and afterwards the visitors would hang around, queuing to peer down a tube at his mum and ask her the same inane questions, while their kids ran riot in the car park or hung around the shop, trying to spend their pocket money on souvenir T-shirts, pencils, rubbers and key fobs bearing pictures of his mum lying in her *box*. Afterwards there would be a mountain of litter all over the car park and he'd be roped into going round with a litter-picker, to the amusement of any kids at school who recognised him. *No, thanks*, Jordan thought. He wasn't that much of a mug.

Instead he was at home replaying the video that his dad had made on the day his mum had been buried: Saturday 26 July – her birthday!

'What a nice way to celebrate the day you came into

the world!' his gran had said, ironically, when Jordan had told her.

She and Chrissie had refused to go near the place, but Jordan and the rest of the family had gone up the day before to watch the hole being dug and the septic tank being delivered. It was massive but, as his dad had pointed out, it had to last his mum five months.

There had been endless discussions at home about how his mum would manage to go to the toilet – or as people at school put it, 'Where on earth does she take a leak? Or a dump?'

Kyle had suggested that if she'd been a man, like Grandpa, she could have managed with a pop bottle and a few plastic carrier bags, as he'd done. Thank goodness his mum had never considered that possibility. Jordan, for one, had made it quite clear he was having nothing to do with disposing of anyone's crap. As it turned out, he'd ended up having to take care of Jet's, but a dog's was different to your mum's!

In the end they'd had to pay extra money to have the hole dug several feet deeper and a septic tank put in first. A trapdoor was fitted in the base of the box that opened onto it. Unlike Annad, who loved that sort of thing, Jordan could hardly bring himself to think about it all. It was no wonder to him that his mum got constipated from time to time; in her place he probably would too.

When they had all gone up to the farm on that first morning, right after his mum's birthday breakfast, they had been surprised by how many people were already there. His aunt and uncle had put up streamers, balloons and banners. Someone had even organised a brass band. There were over twenty TV crews from as far away as Australia and Japan. Ronnie King, a reporter on the local paper, had been there with a photographer, as well as lots of other journalists from the national newspapers. The atmosphere felt like Christmas and several birthdays all rolled into one.

His mum had been in a great mood, laughing and signing autographs. He'd been excited, too. Watching the video, he could see that he hadn't looked worried or upset or sad at all; it really hadn't sunk in yet. It had just felt like a big excuse for a party. He'd had his photo taken loads of times; people were even asking for *his* autograph.

Once the hole was officially measured and pronounced deep enough, the box had been lowered into it. Then everyone had got really excited and there had suddenly been lots more photos: everyone had wanted one taken with his mum.

Next they had lowered in the few things his mum was going to need. His dad had already laid the cables to supply the power for the TV, the lamp, a charger for her mobile phone, and an alarm that was connected up to his uncle and aunt's bedroom, in case his mum had any emergencies.

By midday it had been time for her to get in, and the reporters had called for Jordan to have his final hug – in front of the cameras, of course. He could see now how embarrassed he'd been, because he hadn't been able to think of any last thing he might want to say to her, not with all those people watching them, but he could remember her whispering to him, 'I love you, Jordie.' And then he had been whisked away so she could have a last hug on camera with his dad. People had been crowding closer until there was a real risk that someone was going to fall into the hole, and everyone had been made to move back.

The next bit had happened really quickly: she'd got into the box, had a final photo, then lain down before the lid was lowered on top. At the time it hadn't felt too strange for Jordan, seeing his mum lying in the box. After all, for weeks he'd been coming home from school and taking her up a cup of tea while she'd been practising in it.

A couple of men had got into the hole and started hammering the box lid closed, but the noise had almost been drowned out by all the cheering. Then the two pipes had been fitted, at the head and at the foot, and fixed in place while he and his brother and his dad had been given spades to begin shovelling the soil on top. Jordan often wondered what that must have sounded like to his mum: the soil hitting the box. It still made him shudder. It was one of the things that often featured in his nightmares, that and the deafening sound of a lid being hammered down.

Jordan shook the thoughts away. He idly pressed rewind on the remote and watched the soil reform into heaps around the top of the hole...the lid raise up...his mum climb out...hug his dad, then hug him. Jordan paused for a while before he pressed play and he watched her hug him again...climb down...the lid close...the soil pour in. He paused...dug her up again...brought her to the surface...watched her rise as if from the dead. He'd done this so many times he seriously thought he might wear out the tape. If only he could physically bring his mum back as easily.

The sob that suddenly escaped surprised Jordan; it was enough to wake Jet from his sleep under the TV. The dog came over and licked Jordan's hands. Jordan sighed and absently stroked Jet's head as he finished watching the video.

It had all seemed such a happy day; no one looked in the least bit worried or nervous. But by nine in the evening, when people had started to leave, his mum had had her first panic attack. She'd said she wanted to come out, but somehow his dad and Kyle had managed to calm her down. His dad had stayed all through that first night, after Kyle had taken Jordan home.

Jordan hadn't known any of this at the time. His mum had admitted it to him only much later, but by then she had started sleeping through the night and it had been him who'd begun getting the bad dreams. That was when they had got Jordan a puppy.

'Maybe now he'll stop feeling sorry for himself,' he'd overheard his brother saying.

But Jordan hadn't stopped worrying about his mum, or feeling sorry for himself – he'd just stopped telling anyone. And as the weeks went by, if he'd ever felt tempted to complain, there was always an answer: *the worst part's over...we're more than half way...only six weeks now...a month...sixteen days...almost there.*

Jordan had got into the habit of only complaining to his friends. At home he'd just turned a bit sullen; but then he was thirteen, and according to his dad, at his age lots of boys became silent and uncommunicative.

Jordan was suddenly feeling hungry. He got up and looked in the fridge, although he already knew what was in there: half a leftover pizza. His dad and Kyle would be eating roast dinners up at the farm, as he could have been. He'd had the choice, but Jordan was sick of choices that felt like no choice at all. He didn't want a boring day-old pizza, but he didn't want dinner at the funny farm either.

As if in answer to his prayers, the phone rang. It was his gran calling to see how he was doing.

'You seemed so flat, duck, when you were round on Friday. D'you want to come for lunch?'

Jordan didn't hesitate. 'Yeah. I'm on my way,' he said. And he didn't stop to care who it might upset.

Chrissie was at her boyfriend's when he got there and Jordan thought it was even nicer that it was just him and his gran for a change. After the usual questions about school and what kind of weekend he'd had, Jordan steered the conversation round to talking about his grandpa. He loved talking to his gran about him.

'How did you first meet?' he wanted to know. 'Weren't you still at school?

'That's right,' his gran told him. 'We were regular childhood sweethearts. Of course we couldn't get married until he was twenty-one, and he'd done his national service. I was only eighteen when I got married.'

That was Chrissie's age, and to Jordan it seemed so young. Only five years older than he was!

'And then it wasn't long before babies came along, first your Uncle Matt, then your mum. She was an odd one, your mum,' his gran went on. 'Even as a little one, she was fiercely independent, always her daddy's girl. And stubborn – as a mule – just like him.' His gran got up and started to clear the plates away. 'It's one thing for a man to do something like that, but I don't understand how Debbie could,' she said. '*Abandoning* you all for so long.'

Jordan felt this was a bit extreme. 'It's not been that long,' he countered.

'*Five months!* Nearly half a year – it's a lot out of your childhood. She's selfish, plain selfish, just like her father.'

His gran looked so cross. Jordan wanted to argue with her, felt he ought to defend his mum, but part of him agreed with her. Why was she doing it, if she really did care about him? It was the question he'd been asking himself a lot lately.

His mobile suddenly went off and he knew without looking that it would be her. He took the call, but walked into the kitchen, pretending the reception might be better there.

'Hello, sweetheart,' his mum said. 'Are you OK?'

'Yeah,' Jordan replied, a touch of *why wouldn't I be?* in his tone.

'What've you had for lunch?'

'Not much, I wasn't hungry,' Jordan lied.

'You've got to eat,' his mum said. 'I don't want to find you've wasted away when I get out. Never mind, we'll have such a big, slap-up meal when I come home. I can't wait.'

At the moment his mum had to be careful what she ate because she was getting no exercise. The doctor had given her a diet to follow and his Aunt Julie made sure she kept to it. But his mum had a real sweet tooth and was always asking Jordan to bring her a Mars Bar, even though his dad had made him promise not to.

'Are you coming up to see me later?' she asked. Jordan hesitated. 'It's OK if you're busy, duck. Your dad said you'd got lots of homework to do. We don't want you falling behind at school.'

Now Jordan felt even more guilty. He'd lied to his dad *and* his mum, and he still hadn't opened his school bag. At the beginning he'd gone up to the farm every day, sometimes before school and after. Soon it got to be just once a day, and now it was only when he felt like it, or when he couldn't find a good enough excuse not to go. He spoke to his mum every day on the phone, but that was mainly because she rang him; it didn't involve any effort on Jordan's part.

He started to itch. His eczema had been pretty quiet for the last month, but recently he'd noticed it starting up again. He hadn't even been aware he was scratching until his mum said, 'Jordan, are you still there? Are you scratching?'

He wondered how she could possibly tell. He sighed and changed the subject. 'I was just thinking what I'd got on tomorrow. Look, I'll come up after school,' he promised, partly to appease his guilt, partly to distract her from his eczema.

'That'd be great,' she said. 'I miss you, you know.'

'I miss you too, Mum,' he replied.

'Look after that eczema; you don't want a flare-up.'

'Yeah, yeah...' he said.

'It's Monday,' she reminded him, 'so it must be cooking. Have you got everything you need?'

'Yeah, gotta go, Mum. See you tomorrow.'

When he ended the call, his gran was standing right

behind him. He wondered if she'd heard him lying about food, deliberately letting his mum think he was at home, rather than at her house.

But if she had heard, she didn't mention it.

'I'll see you Friday, my darling,' she said, giving him a peck on the cheek. 'Keep your chin up. It'll all be over soon.'

CHAPTER SEVEN

He had no idea where he was. It was too dark to see anything and he was too scared to move in order to find out. He could feel that he was in a corner – crouching – hard surfaces on all sides. But when he tentatively reached out his hands he could feel things moving, the walls slowly closing in on him, pushing him tighter and tighter into the corner...forcing the breath out of him until he felt as if he was suffocating...

Jordan woke himself up, wrestling his way out of his bedclothes. He lay there with his eyes wide open, reassuring himself that he was actually safe at home in his own bed. When he checked the time it was still early, but he knew he wouldn't get back to sleep now. For once he wouldn't need to be late for school. Jordan lay scratching his arms and legs, not even aware he was doing it. He was thinking about the day ahead. It was Monday, which meant maths, geography, chemistry and then a whole afternoon of home economics. Could be worse. At least he'd have a good laugh with his friends all afternoon. Anand and cookery was always a pretty hilarious combination.

Their home economics teacher was called Mrs Batty, which was a source of amusement to all her classes, especially because she *was* quite forgetful – a bit of a handicap for a cookery teacher. It meant that the smoke alarms frequently went off and there was often a smell of over-baked or even burnt food in the room.

Personally, Jordan wished Mrs Batty could have been a bit more forgetful, particularly when it came to his eczema. All the teachers had been notified of his condition and warned that contact with certain substances or foods *could* irritate matters. Mrs Batty was zealous on the matter and not prepared to take any chances. If they were actually handling any food – as they were today – she would insist Jordan wore gloves and sometimes other protective gear. He'd had this struggle with her time and again, and Jordan never won.

'I don't need them, honest, Miss. It's fine. I haven't had any trouble for weeks,' he lied.

'Not worth risking a flare-up though, is it, Jordan?' she insisted.

Now Anand stood nearby, laughing, and waving a wooden spoon in the air, as Jordan was forced to put on a pair of latex gloves and a coverall. Martine looked away, smirking, pretending to check their ingredients against the recipe card.

Jordan held his temper until the teacher moved on to harass some other poor sucker and he was free to ditch the gloves and the coverall.

'*Don't!*' he warned, as Anand opened his mouth, but his friend couldn't help himself.

'You looked like one of the dinner ladies there for a minute. You just needed the hairnet.'

Jordan grabbed his own wooden spoon and the two boys were soon mock-fencing.

'Oh, welcome to the infants' table,' Martine said, wearily, then confiscated the spoons before Mrs Batty could turn and catch them.

Today they were making bread buns. The three friends stood in a row at a bench, each mixing their ingredients. As she finished hers, Martine looked over into Anand's bowl and asked whether he'd bothered washing his hands before he'd started. Anand looked first at his own dough and then at his friends'. Theirs was the same creamy colour, while his own was a grubby shade of grey.

He shrugged; too late now.

'Just don't blame us if you die of food poisoning,' Martine said, helpfully.

They added the liquid and started to knead the dough. Mrs Batty had demonstrated the technique and told them that you couldn't really overdo the kneading, which had been a bit of a mistake because Anand was now treating his dough like a punch-bag.

'You're supposed to be kneading it, not murdering it,' Martine told him.

But Anand was enjoying himself far too much to take any notice. When he'd finally used up all his energy and his frustration, and while his friends finished kneading their dough, Anand filled them in on his dad's latest disaster scenario...

Because he was completely convinced that the price of fuel was going through the roof, his father had been out and bought up a job lot of calor gas cylinders.

'I wouldn't mind, but he's storing them all in my room and I have to climb over them to get into bed. *"You will thank me, ungrateful boy,"*' Anand mimicked his father, '*"when all the world is shivering and you are cosy as toast."*'

Jordan hadn't any new developments to share with the others, but Martine told them, with some satisfaction, that her sister's friend, who was making the bridesmaids' dresses, had asked for a lot of extra money because of the number of alterations she'd had to make to Martine's.

'I told my mum this diet isn't working and maybe I should come off it, but she pretended she was deaf.'

'Maybe you've got something wrong with your glands,' Jordan suggested. 'I certainly never heard of anyone eating less and getting fatter.'

Jordan was so busy kneading he missed the look that passed between Martine and Anand, but he couldn't miss the fight that broke out a moment later when they started breaking off tiny bits of dough and flicking them at one another.

'Now who're the infants?' he asked, at which the others turned on him and he suddenly came under a hail of bread dough pellets that only stopped short when the teacher homed in on them.

The dough, or what was left of it, was finally formed into bread buns, and placed on trays in the oven. While the buns cooked, everyone tidied up – or stood around watching his friends do it, in Anand's case.

'I wish they'd hurry up and cook. I'm starving,' Jordan said. Despite being in plenty of time today he'd skipped breakfast again.

But Martine, who was also feeling hungry, snapped, 'At least you're not on a stupid diet.'

'I might as well be,' Jordan snapped back. 'There's no food in our house most of the time.' Repeating his gran's words he added, 'I don't understand how my mum could be so selfish.'

'Selfish!' Martine asked, open-mouthed. 'What do you mean, selfish?'

'What she's doing: taking herself off, leaving us to fend for ourselves.'

'Selfish?' Martine repeated. 'You should come to my house; I'll show you selfish. At least what your mum's doing is a blow for women's lib.'

'How d'you make that out?' Anand asked.

'She's showing that a woman can do anything a man can do. What she's doing takes guts. I really admire your mum,' she said, more seriously now. 'She's not starving herself like mine, trying to look like a country and western Barbie doll. At least there's some point to what your mum's doing.'

'Lying in a coffin for five months! Where's the point in that?' Jordan demanded. 'There'd be some point if she was cycling round the world for cancer, or tight-rope walking even. I could understand it better if she was setting a world record for anything else.' He searched for something that was less passive... 'Spitting, even.'

'Spitting?' Martine said. 'That's gross.'

'Not that kind of spitting,' Jordan snapped. 'They spat cherry stones or something. The point is, at least they were *doing* something!'

This was what really rankled for Jordan: the fact that his mum was doing *nothing* and yet it was taking her so long to do it. That's what he couldn't forgive.

Jordan was still thinking about all this when he rode up to the farm later that afternoon. He was relieved to find the place pretty quiet. It was a cold grey December day and beginning to get dark, so it was probably not too surprising that there were hardly any cars in the car park.

Jordan propped up his bike and waved to his aunt, who was in the café. She called him over and he hoped she was going to offer him a big piece of cake, or a toasted teacake, or a Danish pastry – maybe all three.

'How was school?' she asked.

Jordan shrugged. Why, he wondered, did adults always ask that question? Did they imagine school was the only thing going on in a kid's life?

His aunt gave him a flask of coffee to deliver to his mum, a can of Coke for himself, and told him to take whatever he wanted from the tray of cakes. It was a disappointingly thin choice. She quickly explained that they'd had a coach party through earlier that had almost cleaned her out. Being quite close to the M1, his aunt's café had become a convenient tea stop for coach trips going north or south – with the added attraction of a visit to *the woman in a box*.

Jordan took a chocolate cookie and had finished it before he even reached the door.

'*Thank you*,' his aunt prompted him.

'Yeah, thanks,' Jordan mumbled between bites.

'Coffee coming down, Mum,' he called, before lowering the flask in the hook-a-duck. He also put in one of his bread buns. He'd eaten all the rest before he got there; even without any butter they didn't taste half bad.

'Hello, love,' his mum called back up. She sounded

as if she'd just woken from a nap. 'How was…' she started.

'Usual.' Jordan cut her off.

'Mmm, coffee, lovely, and…a bread bun?'

'We made them today at school,' he told her.

'Mmm, delicious,' she said, biting into it. 'So what's new?'

'Nothing,' Jordan said. 'Dad still isn't doing enough shopping, so there's never anything to eat.' The cookie had barely touched the sides of his stomach.

'Have you told him?'

'I never *see* him,' Jordan complained. 'He's always up here.'

'When he's not at work or looking after you,' his mum corrected him.

'Yeah, whatever.'

'Someone sounds a bit of a grizzly bear. Is your rash bothering you again?'

'*Nooo!*' Jordan snapped, but suddenly realised he had started to scratch again.

Picking up his mood, his mum made the mistake of trying to jolly Jordan along. 'Won't be long now, only fifteen days…'

This only made him more irritable. 'Mum,' he demanded, 'what do you find to do all day?'

His mum laughed. 'You know very well what I do.' She started to list her daily regime. 'When I first wake up I have to do my exercises…'

Jordan knew about those. They weren't like anything you'd do in a gym, but they were all his mum could manage in the space she had. If she kept them up, a few times a day, though, they were meant to help to keep the blood flowing and avoid muscle wastage.

'Then I have a wash and brush up…'

She tried to be scrupulous about cleaning her teeth and washing herself all over, he knew that. For someone who wasn't especially fussy about his own hygiene, Jordan still found it hard to imagine not having a bath or a shower for months on end. He didn't even want to think about the toilet business and sincerely hoped she wasn't going to enlighten him on that subject.

'After I've had my breakfast,' his mum continued, 'I write my diary…'

'What on earth d'you find to write about?' Jordan asked.

'How I feel, the things I think about, the funny questions people ask me.' He knew his mum was hoping to publish this diary one day. It would certainly be unique, she'd argued. But Jordan couldn't imagine who on earth would be interested, when nothing at all happened day after day after day.

'I watch TV for a bit,' she went on, 'but I prefer looking at my photos. I try to remember when they were taken, where we were and what we were all doing at the time.' She began to sound a bit wistful.

Jordan could tell from her voice that she was probably missing them as much as they were missing her, and he realised that she had so much more time to feel that stuff. But that just made him even angrier because, unlike him, his mum had a choice. 'If you stopped being so selfish and pulled yourself together and got yourself out of there you wouldn't have to look at photos,' he wanted to tell her. 'You could see us for real.' But Jordan knew he couldn't say that. He wasn't allowed to.

'Well, I can tell you, I'd be bored out of my skull,' he said instead.

'No, you wouldn't,' she argued, 'because there's always someone wanting to talk to you, all these visitors to entertain. Sometimes I just wish they'd go away and give me a bit of peace.'

'But what on earth do you tell them?' Jordan was completely exasperated by now. 'It's not like you're *doing* anything down there.'

His mum picked up his tone and, sounding a little exasperated herself, said, 'I'm setting a world record, Jordan!'

Jordan sighed. There wasn't really any answer to that. For a while, an awkward silence followed before his mum broke it.

'And, as well as that,' she said more lightly, 'I still find time to keep my eye on you, young man, and what you're up to. Anyway, in case you've forgotten, it's only six days before I pass the present record. Have you invited your friends to the party? Dad says he's organised fireworks.'

'Yeah,' Jordan said, without enthusiasm.

They'd had a party, but a smaller one, when his mum had passed his grandpa's record of 100 days. It had been the week before Bonfire Night, so they'd had a few fireworks then too. But he knew from all of his dad's plans that this was going to be a *much* bigger affair. On Sunday his mum would set her own world record of one hundred and forty-one days, then she would be in the record books. She would be famous. It was a real achievement – even Jordan had to admit that.

He suddenly felt guilty about being so bad tempered. It *was* a huge deal to his mum and he ought to try to feel happier for her. The party would be a laugh for him and his friends and hopefully at this one he could get lost in the crowd – not like his birthday party. Just thinking about that had Jordan starting to itch.

Back in October he'd turned thirteen and it had been the worst birthday of his life. They'd had the party up at the farm. His aunt had made a cake and pizza and stuff and they'd all stood around in their coats, some people huddled under umbrellas because it was raining, just so his mum could join in when they sang 'Happy Birthday' to him.

She'd been going through another tough patch round about then and when she thought about missing Jordan's birthday she'd got quite weepy. So his dad had decided to make a big deal out of it. He'd invited lots of people, including that idiotic reporter, Ronnie King, and his stupid sidekick, Colin the camera, as Jordan had nicknamed him. The only thing more brainless than the kind of poses Colin had tried to get Jordan into were the questions Ronnie King had asked him: *How does it feel having a mum buried underground? Are you missing her? Do you think you'd like to do the same when you grow up?*

And finally, after Jordan had blown out his candles: *So, do you want to tell us your birthday wish, Jordan?*

– just as if he were three years old. He was tempted to tell the reporter, 'I wish you were buried down there, instead of my mum, but without any tubes to talk through!'

The final straw had been when his dad had got his birthday present wrong: the pair of trainers he'd been wanting for weeks, but two sizes too small. It was so embarrassing. His mum would never have done that.

Jordan comforted himself that at least there wouldn't be a repeat of that embarrassing ordeal when it came to Christmas. They wouldn't be opening presents standing over his mum's grave in the rain. By Christmas everything would be back to normal. She'd be out in time to buy his presents, to cook the dinner. Everyone would be back together again. It was this thought of a proper Christmas, with a reunited family, that was keeping Jordan going.

He'd asked his dad a few days earlier about buying the tree and getting down the box of decorations from the loft, but his dad had said, 'There's plenty of time for that, Jordan. We've got more important things to think about right now, like getting your mum through the next couple of weeks. Don't you worry, it's going to be a Christmas to remember. We'll all have plenty to celebrate.'

He knew his dad was right; for the time being Christmas could wait. His mum was so close to her goal now. After next Sunday's party it really would be countdown time. Jordan told himself he could hang in there another two weeks. He could manage that for his mum. Of course he could. Fourteen days? It was nothing.

CHAPTER EIGHT

Despite Jordan's resolution – to think positively – the rest of the week dragged. But finally it was Thursday – almost the end of another week.

Morning break was over, but Jordan and his friends were sitting on tables in the IT room, in no hurry to move, because Mr Squires, their IT teacher, was always the last to leave the staffroom.

Jordan had been telling his friends about the party on Sunday: the fireworks, the TV crews, the free food and drink.

'G-reat,' Anand responded. 'I'm up for a party.'

'Party? Whose party? We'll come.' Jason Carlisle and his crew crashed into their conversation.

'Yeah, we'll be there,' Nutter Norris agreed.

'Jordan's mum, on Sunday,' Anand told them. 'She's setting a new world record. There's gonna be fireworks and everything.'

Jordan and Martine looked away, cringing yet again at the way Anand behaved around the footie crew. Why did he always try too hard?

Martine, as usual, completely ignored the boys' interruption and returned to the conversation. 'Oh, so it's OK now,' she tackled Jordan, 'now your mum's about to get really famous? It's not such a totally pointless exercise any more?'

'I didn't say that, exactly,' he started to hedge. He wasn't going to be pushed into defending his mum, but he was trying not to undermine her either.

Jason Carlisle came and sat on the corner of their table and remarked in a general kind of way, 'It's gotta be pretty gross talking to your mother down a drainpipe.'

'I don't remember anyone asking *your* opinion,' Martine told him. Apart from Jordan and Anand, who she treated as exceptions, she had a generally low opinion of boys, especially the footie crew.

'It's gotta be even more gross if you're at the bottom of the drainpipe,' the Biscuit sneered.

'Yeah, never knowing what's gonna drop on your head,' Nutter Norris grinned. 'Per-lop!'

The three boys were right in Jordan's face. He could tell where this conversation was headed; he'd been there too many times before.

'Hey, Gibbo, what's the weirdest thing anyone ever dropped down on her?'

Jordan had gradually turned away from them, until he was facing the windows, but the boys followed him, determined to stay right in his face.

'Chewie, cigarette ends, the odd condom?' Jason Carlisle suggested. The other boys were laughing and, to Jordan's dismay, even Anand joined in.

'Just shut up, Carlisle,' Martine told him.

'No, seriously, we're interested,' Jason persisted.

Jordan had been putting up with this kind of ribbing about his mum for so many months: all the snide remarks, usually about the sordid side of it. He'd never had much of a temper, unlike Martine – hers was legendary. Even boys in Year 9 thought twice before provoking her. But Jordan was sick of being the butt of everyone's grubby jokes and he suddenly saw red.

'For God's sake, you morons,' he exploded, 'just get a life, can't you?!' He jumped off the table, hurling a few chairs out of his path.

'Who rattled his cage?' the Biscuit asked no one in particular.

'Go to hell, all of you!' Jordan yelled as he exited the classroom.

Sadly, he didn't get very far because he met Mr Squires halfway down the corridor and was forced to make a humiliating return to his desk, his tail between his legs, with the whole class watching him and most of them jeering.

Throughout the lesson, Jordan kept snatching glances at the footballers, but only once or twice were they looking his way and grinning, and even then not in a particularly pointed way. He felt as if he'd let them push him into making even more of a fool of himself, over nothing at all.

At lunchtime, when he was still brooding over what had happened, Martine told him not to blow it up into anything. 'It's no big deal,' she said. 'Anyone can lose their temper.'

'You should know,' Anand grinned. 'Anyway, it was pretty ace,' he told Jordan. 'I mean...you were impressive, man.'

But it had left Jordan feeling like everyone could see inside him, like he was easy to read, making him even easier to wind up.

Martine must have felt a bit sorry for him because at home time she said, 'I'll come with you, if you're going to see your mum, keep you company.'

That cheered him up and he turned to Anand and asked, 'You coming?'

But the footie crew were waiting for Anand and he stood looking awkward for a moment, before he shrugged and headed over to them. Jordan felt like this was a betrayal and the other boys knew it. They went off grinning, arms round Anand's shoulders. His friend looked to be in seventh heaven.

'He'll never learn,' Martine said, shaking her head.

Jordan wondered why Anand didn't care that the boys were only after the sweets and ciggies, that as soon as they tired of those he'd be out on his ear.

Jordan was glad of Martine's company but he hoped she wouldn't stay too long when they got to the farm, because he wanted some time to talk to his mum on his own. For once, when she asked him how school was, he might even tell her the truth.

But when they reached the farm Jordan could see straight away that wasn't going to happen. The place was heaving. There were two foreign TV crews – one from Spain and one from Japan. The Japanese crew had been there more often than any other. It puzzled Jordan that the Japanese people seemed to be more fascinated with his mum's attempt than any other nation.

He let out a few choice words, under his breath, as he stood on the edge of the car park, trying to decide what to do. It was possible they might all leave soon; it was getting far too dark for filming. He was trying to decide whether to wait to find out.

Just then his Aunt Julie spotted him, and called out, 'There he is. Jordie, come here, duck, and be interviewed.'

That was the last thing in the world he wanted and all he needed to help him decide. 'I'm getting out of here,' he told Martine, climbing onto his bike. 'I'll wait for you on the main road.' Then he turned to his aunt and called, 'Can't stop. See you later.'

Jordan raced off down the track, laughing to himself at his close escape, listening to Aunt Julie calling his name: '*Jordan! Jordan! Wait!*'

When he reached the road, and it felt safe to stop, he waited for Martine to catch up. By the time she reached him she was completely out of breath and mad as a badger.

'What was all that about?' she puffed. 'Leaving me like that?'

'Just forget it,' he told her, then he changed the subject. 'You know, if you took a bit more exercise...'

The look Martine gave him should have warned him off, but Jordan was genuinely beginning to worry. He hadn't really noticed her getting bigger until it was staring him in the face. Now he was starting to feel responsible for her, too. 'You could try getting a bike,' he suggested.

'You could try minding your own flipping business,' she replied.

Jordan finally backed off. He quickly tried to think of a safe subject and finally asked, 'What do you think about all this nicking of Anand's?'

Martine looked at him sharply and then looked away. Jordan couldn't tell whether this indicated that she knew, but hadn't realised *he* knew, or that she didn't know and was shocked by the news.

'Surely you knew?' he said.

Martine shrugged, as if it were no business of hers.

'He's going to be in deep trouble if his dad finds out.'

'Over a few bars of chocolate?'

'It's more than a few,' Jordan snapped. 'And when he finds out about the ciggies...he'd better look out.'

Martine looked as if she were embarrassed by the

109

conversation. Again, Jordan couldn't tell if this was news to her. It wasn't long before they reached her road and she seemed relieved to get away.

'See you tomorrow,' Jordan called after her.

Martine briefly nodded and walked slowly down the road.

Jordan stood watching her for a moment, scratching his arms through his jacket before he cycled on. He felt even more confused now. He was genuinely worried about Anand and he couldn't understand why Martine wasn't. He was starting to feel concerned about Martine too. He didn't feel as if he was any kind of friend to either of them at the moment. No real use to anyone, in truth, and that was a new and uncomfortable feeling for Jordan.

Over supper – barely lukewarm lasagne – Jordan half-listened to his dad and Kyle talking about the plans for Sunday night. Several times they tried to involve him in the conversation, but he was too distracted, thinking about other things.

Out of nowhere, Jordan asked his dad, 'What would you do if you found I'd been stealing from you?'

His dad looked up sharply, but Kyle got in first: 'Knock your block off.'

'Why?' his dad asked. 'Have you been?' It would certainly have been easy enough. His father regularly left money for his mum's shopping and he rarely asked Jordan to account for it, or for the change. Why would he, since he trusted him?

Jordan flushed at the idea. 'No, honest,' he said quickly, 'it was just some boy at school, I heard him bragging about it, that's all. I'd never do anything like that.' He could hear himself trying too hard to convince and turned even redder, desperate for his dad to believe him.

'Well, I'd be very disappointed,' his father said, holding Jordan's eye. '*Very* disappointed.'

Jordan felt almost as guilty as if he had actually stolen, or at least considered it. He was a prize fool. Why on earth had he even brought up the subject? He got up from the table and took his half-eaten food through to the kitchen. After a minute or two his dad followed him and caught him having a secret scratch.

His arms had been driving him mad, and his neck. He'd tried all through supper to keep his hands off the worst spots, which were behind his knees and inside his elbows.

'Don't scratch, lad, it'll only make it worse. What's started that off?'

Kyle called through from the other room, 'If he had a shower once in a while it might help.'

'How long's it been bad?' his dad asked.

Jordan tried to play it down and pretended he'd hardly noticed he was scratching.

'Are you using your cream?'

'I'll go and put some on now,' he said, glad of the excuse to get away before his dad asked to see it and discovered how red and raw it really was. It had been getting worse for days. Jordan had just hoped it would go away, which it never did without the cream.

He went upstairs, stripped off and lay on his bed on top of a towel, wearing only his shorts, letting the cream dry in. As if his life weren't bad enough – without this. Jordan was used to his eczema, he'd had it for years, but right now it felt like the final straw.

His dad called up, 'Jordie, I'm going now. D'you want to come with me?'

But Jordan called back, 'No, thanks. I've got stuff to do.' He knew his dad would assume that meant homework and he was happy to let him think so.

'OK,' his dad replied. 'I'll lock the door behind me. I won't be late.'

Kyle must have already gone to TA. That meant his dad was doing the early shift and would be home by nine. Kyle would take over until ten thirty, which was how they usually worked it. Jordan would be alone for the next couple of hours. He lay looking at the ceiling, his hands securely trapped underneath him. He was feeling *really* sorry for himself, even though he knew it was mainly his own fault. Kyle was right – he hadn't been taking enough showers, or changing his clothes often enough, or resisting scratching, or using the cream at the first signs, or the cotton gloves he was meant to wear in his sleep. All of those things he'd have done – if his mum had been here to remind him.

The cream was beginning to work, or at least it was taking the heat out of it. But he knew it was only temporary relief. He should really get up and find some way to distract himself, but Jordan couldn't even be bothered to move. Instead he lay there, doing the worst thing he could: thinking about it.

He thought about the last really bad flare-up he'd had, a couple of weeks after his birthday in October. That had been the worst ever. He'd scratched his arms so much the rash had got infected and he'd developed impetigo. He'd ended up in hospital for a couple of nights.

Jordan had never been in hospital before. He was ashamed to admit it – after all he was thirteen – but he'd been scared and badly wanted his mum. The doctor had assured them it wasn't serious, but Jordan had to stay in hospital to be given intravenous antibiotics and he needed to be isolated, because impetigo was so infectious.

His dad had stayed – most of the time – but they hadn't wanted to tell his mum until Jordan was better and home again.

'You'll only be here a couple of nights,' his dad had told Jordan. 'I'll stay with you as much as I can, and when I'm not here Kyle will be. I know it's hard and that you probably want your mum, but...' he trailed off.

Jordan knew what he was trying to say: his mum was over halfway.

'If we tell her, she'll be torn in two,' Kyle said.

'Still, it's up to you, Jordie,' his dad had finally said. 'If you really need her...'

He could see his brother watching him, waiting to see if Jordan would act his age, or behave like the baby Kyle often accused him of being. Yet again Jordan felt he had no choice. He didn't want to wreck his mum's chances, but he had wanted to see her – *so badly*.

And that was how he felt now. There was no one else in the house to hear him if he wanted to cry. But he was thirteen, for God's sake. It was *pathetic* – crying over a bit of a rash. Jordan got up and stamped about the room, trying to hold back the tears. Just then his mobile rang, and he knew who it would be. He was tempted to ignore it, but the need to talk to his mum won over. He let her speak first, while he tried to breathe back the tears.

'Hello, Jordie, how are you doing, duck?'

Jordan took another breath, then said, 'OK.' But his mum could clearly sense all the things he wasn't saying.

'Are you feeling a bit low, sweetie?' she asked. 'I've been feeling rather like that today. I did miss talking to you.'

'I came,' Jordan told her, 'but it was...it was a madhouse.'

'Yeah, I know. I'm glad they've all gone home now.'

Jordan didn't speak; he still didn't trust himself to say much.

'Do you want to tell me what it's about?' his mum asked.

Jordan considered lying, but admitted, 'It's just my eczema's bad...'

As soon as the words were out he caught his breath again so as not to cry.

His mum didn't have a go at him about how he'd let it get that bad. Instead she reminded him of all the things that would help now: keeping his cream in the fridge so it was really cool when he used it; wearing his special pyjamas with no seams; having a cool bath before he got into bed. She reminded him about the few drops of lavender oil she sometimes put on his pillow to help him sleep.

Jordan realised that it really wouldn't have mattered what she was saying, just hearing her voice was making it all calm down.

'I'll tell you what,' she said. 'You go and have a bath now, put your cream on, and when you're in bed call me back. OK?'

Jordan got up and went to run a bath. While he was still in it he heard his dad come in. Almost straight away he heard the Hoover going in his bedroom. By the time Jordan came out of the bath, his dad had done the mattress, put clean sheets on his bed, and cleared all his dirty washing off the bedroom floor and hoovered that too. He didn't say a word about any of it to Jordan, but he gave him a big hug before he tucked him in bed.

'Let's try to keep on top of this, Jordie,' he whispered. 'We don't want anything to upset your mum right now, do we, with only eleven days left?'

Eleven days. Finally, it *was* getting closer; even Jordan could see that. He got into bed and phoned his mum. He lay with the phone to his ear while she sang to him. It was a song her dad had sung to her when she was little, and it was what she sang to Jordan if ever he couldn't sleep.

> *My Bonnie lies over the ocean,*
> *My Bonnie lies over the sea...*
> *My Bonnie lies over the ocean.*
> *Oh, bring back my Bonnie to me.*

That night was the first night in a week that Jordan didn't have a bad dream.

CHAPTER NINE

The party had been going on for most of the day. Jordan recognised lots of people from school – some he was glad to see, others he wasn't quite so sure about: a few girls from his class who he knew fancied him had followed him around giggling all day. And there were a few he was definitely *not* glad to see, but for once the footie crew had kept out of his way. Although the two people he really wanted there – his sister and his gran – hadn't come, at least Martine and Anand had made it.

One of the best things about the party was how much food there was. He'd eaten so many burgers his Aunt Julie had told him to go easy. 'You're going to make yourself sick, duck.'

'I've got four months of my dad's cooking to make up for,' he told her, giving her his winning smile.

'Yes, but probably best not to do it all in one day.'

For every burger Jordan had eaten Anand had matched him – and some; but then everybody knew that his friend could have eaten for England. Poor Martine, on the other hand, was barely allowed a bag of crisps by her mum and sister, who'd hardly let her out of their sight. They'd kept offering her a handful of nuts or dried fruit they'd brought along so she wouldn't be tempted. Martine told them she'd rather eat the car park.

She was in possibly the worst mood Jordan had ever seen her. She'd been rather short with him at school after their fall-out on Thursday, but that was nothing compared to the state her family had wound her into today.

'They're so *embarrassing*,' she told Jordan through gritted teeth. 'I wish *they* were down there instead of your mum.'

Jordan also wished it were anyone else's mum down there but his. Today, though, he wasn't going to dwell on that. It wasn't for much longer and he wanted to just enjoy the party. He was beginning to feel more than a bit proud of his mum – *the new world-record holder.*

There had been a great atmosphere all day, with speeches, a champagne toast, and everyone cheering his mum and singing 'For She's a Jolly Good Fellow'. It had got even noisier once people had had a couple of free glasses of champagne.

The champagne had been donated by one of the local businesses that had sponsored his mum: the same company that had made the box she was buried in. They'd brought along a facsimile box so that people could see just how small the space was that she'd existed in for so many months. Some people had taken the opportunity to get into it, lie down, and imagine themselves in her place, but only the very brave ones had allowed the lid to be placed on top. Anand had had a quick go and pretended to go to sleep, but nothing would have induced Jordan to get into it.

By mid-evening, after the fireworks had finished, people began drifting away. Martine had left early in a red-hot temper.

'See you tomorrow,' Jordan and Anand had called after her.

'If I haven't run away by then,' she called back.

It was really cold now and Jordan and Anand went to sit inside the café to warm up a bit. The music was still so loud it was almost making the windows rattle.

There had been so many people there all day, walking over his mum's head, and Jordan wondered what she had made of it. How much could she hear? Could she feel the vibrations all that way down – six feet deep? He suddenly pictured the scene like one of those cross-sections you saw in books, showing layers of soil and rock, with tunnels running through it. He imagined his mum inside the box, and the box sitting inside a small pocket of space, with the solid mass of earth, all six feet of it, on top of her. In his mind she was so small, so vulnerable...

'What's up?' Anand suddenly broke into his thoughts.

Jordan shook his head. 'I was just thinking...it's my mum's party and she's not even here. Doesn't seem fair we're the ones having a good time when she's still down there on her own.'

'Yeah, but she's got the record,' Anand reminded him. 'When she comes out it'll be her name in the record books – not ours.'

Jordan grinned. It was beginning to sink in that his mum had done something no one else in the entire world – in the entire history of the world – had ever done before, and might never do again. They were still waiting to see or hear from someone at *The Guinness*

Book of Records. Technically speaking it would be midnight before they could officially call it a new record, but after almost five months what did a few hours matter?

'Want another burger?' Anand asked.

Jordan shook his head. He felt completely stuffed and wondered where his friend was putting it all. He was reminded of what his grandpa used to say whenever he was that full: 'Couldn't take a message.'

He watched Anand go and get himself a seventh – or was it eighth? – burger of the day. Earlier Jordan had been feeling relieved that things with his friend seemed back to normal, and all the stuff with the footie crew had blown over, but suddenly there they were in his face again – literally. A whole row of them pressed up against the glass making hideous, stupid faces at him. They'd been out there a while, making a nuisance of themselves. In the absence of a football they'd kicked empty beer cans around the car park.

Ricky Doherty's brother was revving up his motorbike and doing wheelies on the gravel. Jordan's Uncle Matt soon put a stop to that and sent the rest of the boys packing. Jordan watched them go off, shouting and kicking up showers of gravel. Ricky Doherty bent and scooped up a few handfuls and threw them against the windows of the café like a shower of hail – not enough to do any damage, just enough to get everyone's attention.

Jordan asked himself why he would possibly want to spend time with any of those morons. 'You want to keep clear of that lot,' he warned Anand, who'd just returned with his food.

Anand shrugged, as if to say, what could he do? It was like Martine always said: Anand couldn't help himself. He was a football junkie – and they were his dealers.

Ronnie King, the reporter, walked into the café with Colin the Camera. Jordan groaned inwardly and looked for a quick exit, but it was too late, they were already approaching the boys' table.

'I wondered where you were hiding,' Ronnie told Jordan.

Jordan had already had his picture taken so many times that day that he'd got face-ache. There'd been so many different reporters he'd found himself answering the same questions over and over again, and he was sick of hearing himself repeat things. At least Ronnie King was harmless. He asked daft questions but he didn't try to bully you. Some of the national reporters had seemed pretty scary to Jordan, and he'd tried to remember his dad's warning to be very careful what he told them.

'They're only after sensationalist rubbish and they'll twist whatever you say until they get it.'

'One last photo and a good quote?' Ronnie asked Jordan. 'Something new?'

Ronnie had been covering his mum's story so long he'd said everything there was to say. Jordan sighed heavily, to let Ronnie know he was doing him a big favour. He could feel his friend nudging his elbow until the penny finally dropped.

'OK,' he told Ronnie, 'but I want my friend in the photo.'

Anand grinned and smoothed down his hair, as if his moment of fame had finally arrived.

The boys wrapped their arms around each other's shoulders and grinned big, cheesy grins. Then, while Colin the Camera took Anand's name and details, Ronnie King asked Jordan, 'So are you proud of your mum's record?'

'Of course I'm proud of her,' Jordan said with a snort. 'Dead proud! She's fantastic.' As he said it, he suddenly felt embarrassed that this wasn't what he'd been telling his friends lately, not even admitting to himself. He remembered what Martine had said about his mum and repeated it to the reporter. 'She's showing that a woman can do anything a man can do – and for far longer.'

Ronnie King looked impressed and scribbled it down. 'So, if someone else comes along and beats your mum's record, do you think that when you're older you'd try to get it back for her – like she's done for your granddad?'

Jordan didn't miss a beat. 'No way,' he said, shaking his head. 'I could never do it. I'm not as brave as my mum.'

Jordan immediately recognised the truth of this. He really did admire her. It didn't matter that he thought it was a stupid thing to want to do – she'd done it, even though she'd had panic attacks. There'd been several times she'd wanted to give up, but she hadn't. Jordan could see what an amazing person his mum was and realised how little he really knew her.

Anand was busy telling Colin the camera that the only record he was interested in was scoring the most goals for Leicester City Football Club. But before anyone could comment on the slim possibility of this ever happening, a row suddenly erupted outside. Jordan looked out of the window and saw his brother having an argument with someone.

They all rushed to the door and Jordan saw Kyle squaring up to one of the reporters. 'You're lying,' he yelled at him.

Jordan heard Ronnie tell Colin that it was Jason Starr, from *The Weekend Sport*. 'I wouldn't want to get in a fight with him,' Ronnie added.

Jordan ran forward and almost collided with his dad, who'd just raced over to pull Kyle away; a couple of other men were trying to reason with the reporter.

'Keep away, lad,' his dad advised, pushing Jordan back. 'Leave it to me.'

But Jordan stayed close by. He hadn't realised quite how big and strong his brother had become. He was almost seventeen and looked like a full-grown man – and with all the training he did...

When Kyle suddenly pulled his arm free of his dad and landed a punch on the reporter's jaw, Jordan heard the crack and it made him feel sick. He was scared. He'd never been so close to a fight; not one between grown men, at least. He felt tears coming and quickly rubbed them away. He didn't want to look like a baby, not at a time like this.

His brother's punch was the only one that actually connected. The fight was soon over, but it had killed the party atmosphere stone dead. Jordan was feeling confused. 'What's happened, Dad?' he asked, but his dad didn't answer him. He was too busy restraining Kyle, who was still pulling away.

But Kyle heard Jordan and answered, 'It's that creep. He said the record's no good. He said she's wasted her time. He's a rotten liar!' he snarled.

But the reporter was sticking to his story. 'It's the truth. They're not going to put it in. They said it's too risky.'

Quite a crowd had gathered and surrounded the reporter, who was looking a little nervous.

'Look, I'm only the messenger,' he told everyone. 'It wasn't my decision. I've been trying all day to get someone from *The Guinness Book of Records* to check it out.' He waved his mobile phone. 'I just got the call. It's definite: they're dropping a few endurance attempts – like this one. They don't want to encourage *dangerous feats*.'

'So it definitely won't get in?' Jordan's dad asked, unable to quite believe his own ears.

'No, it won't get in,' the reporter confirmed.

There was a stunned silence as they all took in the news. Gradually word went round until everyone who was still there had heard it – everyone except Jordan's mum. No one was in a hurry to break the news to her.

Kyle didn't think she should be told, and said so. 'What's to be gained? It won't change anything. It'll only upset her, and where's the point in that when she's only got ten days to go?'

'But what's the point of going on at all?' his uncle asked – exactly echoing Jordan's thoughts. 'She's done what she set out to do.'

'She's beaten the world record,' Aunt Julie agreed. 'Why go on *any* longer…'

'…if it's not going to get in the book,' Jordan said, finishing her sentence for her. But his dad pulled him away from the group.

'Look, I want you to go and say goodnight to your mum,' he told him. 'Just behave normally. Don't say a word about this. I'm going to get Kyle to take you and Anand home. Get yourself to bed; I'll be back late.'

'Are you going to tell her, though, Dad?' Jordan asked.

He nodded. 'I'll have to. But I want to wait till everyone else has gone. I can't imagine what she's going to feel about it.'

'What do you think she'll do?'

His dad shook his head, 'I really don't know, lad.'

Jordan went to tell his mum he was leaving. She sounded as if she'd been dropping off. It had been a pretty busy day for her.

'That's right, duck, you've got school tomorrow,' she told him. 'Have you had a nice time, though?'

'Yeah, great, Mum,' Jordan replied. 'Everyone's heading off now. I'll see you tomorrow. And, Mum...well done. I'm dead proud of you.'

'Thanks, sweetheart. I'm pretty proud of myself.'

Jordan and Kyle got a lift most of the way home with someone from their street. They dropped Anand off, then walked the last hundred metres in silence. Kyle had been ready for a fight that had been over before it began. Now he looked ready for another one. Jordan knew better than to push his luck, but the question burst out of him anyway. 'What do you think she'll do?'

'What do you mean?' Kyle snapped. 'She'll finish what she's started.'

'But it's like Aunt Julie said, what's the point now?'

'Because...it's-what-she-set-out-to-do.' Kyle said it as if he were talking to someone with half a brain. 'One hundred and fifty days! That's ten days to go. Surely you can do the maths?'

They got into the house and Jordan still couldn't let it go. 'But if it's not even going to be in the record book...'

'*Go to bed*,' his brother ordered him.

As Jordan went upstairs he heard Kyle muttering, 'I don't see any point in telling her, personally.'

Jordan lay in bed, his mind in turmoil. He'd tried hard all day to be pleased for his mum, to feel proud of her and her achievement. He really thought he'd got his head round the ten days she still had left. But the moment he heard the news about her record not being included, his first thought hadn't been for her – and how disappointed *she* would be – it had been for himself.

Now, he had begun to think, *surely she'll come out*. Now he would get her back early – maybe even tomorrow. It wasn't out of the question.

CHAPTER TEN

Jordan woke the next morning, surprised to find himself eager to get out of bed – on a school morning, too. He hadn't woken from either a bad dream *or* to his mum's wake-up call. As he remembered the events of the night before, a small sense of hope lit up the room like a sudden burst of sunshine. Jordan knew he was probably being completely stupid, but he held on to his fantasy that when he went down to the kitchen this morning, he'd find his mum sitting at the table.

He knew it wasn't really possible; it would have taken hours to dig her out. No one was going to do that job overnight – but it wasn't *completely impossible.*

In order to hold onto his fantasy a while longer,

he went and had a shower, brushed his teeth, even put on clean clothes. When he finally went into the kitchen, he wasn't too surprised to find his mum not there, but he *was* surprised to find his dad and brother. It was unusual to have any company at breakfast.

Jet rushed forward for his usual morning fuss.

'Down, Jet,' his dad said, half-heartedly.

His dad was looking very tired, as you'd expect of someone who'd been up most of the night, but Jordan thought he looked a whole heap better than Kyle. His brother was not a drinker, and the combination of a few unaccustomed beers and the fight had left Kyle looking as if he'd slept under a hedge. When Jordan learned that his brother had missed his daily training run he knew how bad he must be feeling.

'Morning,' Jordan said, trying to keep his face from giving away what he'd privately been praying for.

'Morning,' his dad responded. 'You look like you've turned over a new leaf.'

Jordan smiled. 'Any chance of a fry up?' he asked hopefully.

'In your dreams,' Kyle replied. He looked as if the thought of a fried breakfast was enough to make his stomach heave.

'It's Monday morning!' his dad reminded him. 'Eat some of that cereal I keep buying you.'

Jordan sat down and poured himself a bowlful. His dad was nursing a cup of coffee; Kyle had something fizzing in a glass.

'Aren't you going to work today?' Jordan asked his dad, still trying to keep the hope out of his voice.

'Yeah, I'm just going in a bit late,' his dad yawned.

Jordan let a few more moments pass while he ate a couple of mouthfuls, before asking, as casually as he could manage, 'How did Mum take the news?'

His dad nodded his head from side to side. 'She's going to be OK. But it was a terrible shock. I hated having to tell her it had all been for nothing.'

'It hasn't been *for nothing*,' Kyle insisted. 'She's still got the record; nobody can take that away from her, whether those idiots put it in the book or not.' He was still so mad he could hardy keep his anger under control. 'I could have killed that reporter. He just couldn't wait to tell us – the smarmy rat.'

'Yeah, well, his timing was bad,' their dad agreed. He got up and pushed two pieces of bread into the toaster. 'But like he said, it wasn't his decision.'

Jordan waited a few more moments before asking, 'So what's she gonna do?'

'What do you mean *do*? Why d'you keep asking that?' Kyle snapped at him.

Jordan's dad returned to the table with two slices of toast, which he buttered before sliding the plate in front of Jordan. 'We'll have to see.'

'You can't let her give up, Dad,' Kyle insisted.

'It's up to her now. She said she wanted to sleep on it.'

Jordan went on eating, as if his dad's words were of no special interest to him, but he couldn't keep it up for long. He left the table and grabbed Jet's lead. 'Better get the dog walked,' he said.

'Sit down,' his dad told him, 'and eat your toast first.'

Jordan folded the two rounds into a couple of sandwiches, grabbed his jacket and said, 'I'll eat them on the way. See you later.' He couldn't get out of the house quickly enough.

So there was still a chance. Jordan felt sure his mum would make the right decision. She'd probably been waiting for an excuse like this. There'd be no shame in giving up now; she'd broken the record. One hundred and fifty days was just a random number she'd plucked out of the air. Realistically, he knew it might take a couple of days, maybe the rest of the week, for his dad to make the arrangements to dig her out, but she could be home by the weekend!

Jordan jogged round the block, almost dragging Jet along with him, hardly allowing the poor dog to enjoy the delights of the different lampposts. He made sure Jet had time for the essentials, but the moment he'd *emptied the tank*, as Jordan liked to put it, he rushed him home, promising the dog a much longer walk later.

When he got back his dad was ready to leave. 'I'll give you a lift, if you're quick.'

'Are you going up to see Mum first?' he asked.

'No, I'm leaving her to have a lie-in this morning,' his dad smiled. 'No pun intended.'

Jordan said thanks, but he'd rather take his bike. He watched his dad drive away and then, as soon as he'd packed his bag for school, set off too. He had to see his mum first. He knew he could have rung her mobile, which would have been quicker, but part of him was putting off finding out. He didn't want his hopes dashed – not just yet.

The farm shop car park looked like the morning after the night before. There was litter everywhere: cans, paper napkins, sweet wrappers, dead fireworks. There was no sign of life from the bungalow. The barrier hadn't been lifted yet. There was room to squeeze his bike round it, but Jordan left it outside rather than push it across the gravel and alert his aunt. He didn't want to talk to her this morning.

He saw that the turnstile carried the sign *'Debbie's sleeping. Do not Disturb'*, but that was for visitors; it didn't apply to him. He climbed over the turnstile and called down, 'Hey, Mum. It's me.'

There was no reply and his good sense should have told him his mum must still be asleep. But he couldn't wait all day to find out what she'd decided. He called a little louder, but tried not to startle her.

'Mu-u-m, are you awake?'

He finally heard her voice. 'Jordan? Is that you? What's the time?'

'Half eight. Are you OK? Hey, Mum, I'm so sorry about *The Guinness Book of Records*. You must be gutted.'

He strained to hear what she said next, but then realised she was yawning and not talking at all. The pipe was too long to have a quiet conversation.

'Has your dad gone to work?' she finally asked.

'Yeah. He's just left.'

'He must have been tired.'

'Yeah,' Jordan laughed, 'but he didn't look half as

rough as Kyle after his f-f...' Jordan quickly swallowed the word *fight* before it left his mouth. He knew they wouldn't want his mum to know about that.

'After what?'

'His...f-friends gave him a couple of beers,' Jordan quickly improvised.

'I feel a bit hungover myself and I only had that one glass of bubbly. I suppose it was all the excitement...and then the news.'

'I bet you're really disappointed,' he said, trying to sound sympathetic.

'Yeah, I was, but I'm getting my head round it now,' she told him. 'I've still got the world record; nobody can take that away from me. And I'm nearly there.' Jordan was immediately alert to catch her next words. 'Only ten days left – so I'm not going to give up now.'

Jordan had a sudden desire to lie on the floor like a toddler and scream, *'But I want you to give up!'*

'What's ten days more,' she went on, 'when I've done a hundred and forty?'

Jordan was tapping the turnstile with the toe of his trainer. He was so frustrated he really felt like kicking the whole thing over. If he stayed there another minute he knew he would completely lose it.

'I've gotta go, Mum,' he said.

'OK, duck, but come and see me later.'

He jumped over the turnstile and kicked his way across the gravel, making as much noise and as much mess as he could possibly manage. He collected his bike and rode off, almost numb with disappointment.

Jordan was glad he hadn't already confided his pathetic little hopes to anyone else. At least Anand and Martine were sympathetic about *The Guinness Book of Records*' decision.

'It's outrageous!' Martine complained. 'It shouldn't be allowed. They shouldn't just be able to drop a record when someone's in the middle of doing it.'

Anand agreed. 'It stinks, man.'

But as the news went round school, Jordan had the feeling that a few people were secretly pleased that his mum's ordeal had, in some ways, been for nothing.

'What a waste of time,' one or two people said. 'Five months down the tube.' But when they asked, 'Does that mean she's given up now?' Jordan was quick to defend his mum and found himself taking up Kyle's position. 'No! Why would she? She's going to do what she set out to do.'

He was determined not to show any hint of what he was really feeling. And as far as Jordan was concerned, he was putting on a pretty good front, but he couldn't quite control a pulse in his leg that kept jumping and gave him the appearance of someone ready to leap up from his seat and race off at any moment. His conversation was a bit erratic, too.

'You're in a funny mood today,' Anand remarked. 'You been on the happy pills?'

'It's probably all that junk food he ate yesterday,' Martine observed, with more than a hint of envy in her voice. 'He's probably high on E numbers.'

Anand didn't seem to care what Jordan was high on; he wasn't complaining. He just seemed glad to have this more fun-loving version around for a change.

But it was quite an effort for Jordan to keep it up, and he realised his friend had been right when he'd described him as a boring old trout lately. He'd almost forgotten how to have any fun.

Martine could tell there was something going on. Jordan caught her looking at him sideways a couple of times, as if she thought he was very slightly out of control, which was actually exactly how he felt. When Jordan was threatened with another detention, this time from his geography teacher, Miss Marr, Martine told him, 'I should watch your step, buddy. You're skating on thin ice.'

'Oh, lighten up,' he told her. Today, in his present mood, he didn't want anyone bringing him down. But after that she gave him the cold shoulder for the rest of the lesson.

During break Martine's mum sent her a text to tell her she'd be picking her up after school because they had to go shopping for wedding shoes. Martine pulled a face and stuffed her phone angrily back in her jacket pocket, then followed the others into the science block.

Despite the strained relations between them, Martine, Anand and Jordan sat together as usual in chemistry. They'd been mixing some simple solution in a test tubes when Anand got a little over enthusiastic with the shaking and spilled it over Martine's trainers.

'Look out, dumbo,' she told him, about to wipe it off with her hand. But the teacher, Mr Austin, handed her some paper towels and told her to go and clean herself up properly in the cloakroom. Martine gave Anand an accusing look before going off.

Anand grinned at Jordan exactly like a five-year-old who'd just got away with some piece of mischief. Jordan shook his head and grinned back. Suddenly a mobile phone went off close by. Mr Austin quickly looked around for the culprit. It was a strict school rule that mobiles were switched off during lessons. Someone was in for it.

Jordan recognised Martine's ringtone. Her jacket hung over a nearby stool.

'Will *somebody* turn that infernal phone off?' Mr Austin shouted.

Anand was closest but made no move, so Jordan reached over and slipped his hand into Martine's pocket. When he brought it out there was no phone – only what he quickly judged to be half a dozen chocolate wrappers. He glanced at Anand, who quickly looked away.

Mr Austin was still watching him. 'I'm waiting, Gibbons.'

Jordan reached into the other pocket and found the phone, plus more wrappers. He turned it off and everyone went back to work, but not before they'd started to snigger at the evidence of Martine's chocolate stash. The lesson quickly went back to normal – for the rest of the class – but Jordan could hardly believe what he'd seen. When Martine came back into the classroom a chorus of pig-like snorting greeted her, which Mr Austin soon quelled.

'And Martine,' he told her, 'please make sure

your mobile phone is switched off *before* you come into my lessons in future.'

Slightly confused, she walked over to the bench, rolling her eyes comically at Jordan and Anand. When she saw Jordan still holding the sweet wrappers, her face changed to one of hostile resentment.

'So? *So?*' she hissed at him. 'I don't know what you're looking so miserable about. It's my funeral.'

'Two weddings and a funeral, actually,' Anand quipped. The other two seemed to find this quite hilarious; only Jordan couldn't see the joke.

'Did you know about this?' Jordan asked Anand directly.

Anand seemed to have trouble with this simple question, but Martine saved him from agonising over it. 'Of course he knew, Inspector Morse. Where d'you think I got it all from?'

Jordan was awash with feelings. He'd never thought she should waste her time with diets, but given that she seemed to be trying so hard he had done his best to encourage her. So he felt unaccountably angry with Anand for sabotaging her efforts and with Martine for being so stupid. He told her so in no uncertain terms.

'Butt out,' Martine told him again. 'It's none of your business. Why should you care?'

Jordan knew it wasn't actually his business. He quickly realised that what was really bugging him was the fact that his two best friends had been conspiring, for goodness knows how long, and not sharing their secrets with him.

As if to rub it all in, when it came to home economics, Martine told him there wasn't room for him on their bench, even though there plainly was. He spent a miserable, sulky afternoon working alone.

After Martine left with her mum, Jordan caught up with Anand and had another go at him for not backing him up earlier.

'It's up to her,' Anand told him. 'Just leave it, why don't you?'

'But we're supposed to be mates. Why's she been hiding it from me?'

Anand looked at him in disbelief. 'You have to ask that, after the heavy number you laid on her?'

'I was trying to help,' Jordan replied, stung.

'Maybe she doesn't want your help.'

Jordan didn't really believe that. He had no clear idea what kind of help he might have been able to offer Martine, but he knew she couldn't be happy about what she'd been doing, otherwise why would she hide it? He'd been so stupid. Logic should have told him that if she was getting bigger by the day she couldn't really be starving herself. He wondered whether it had been just one day's sweet ration he'd found or several days'.

The fact was, if he'd been a better friend he might well have picked up the clues, but he'd been far too full of his own troubles. He'd dismissed all Martine's grumbling about the wedding because...well, it was girls' stuff, not really anything to get seriously wound up about. But it had been important to her and he should have taken more notice.

He was disappointed with Anand too – the provider of the chocolate, and her other so-called friend.

'Why did you do it?' he asked him now.

It was a simple enough reason for Anand. 'Because she asked me; I'm her mate, not her mother,' he told Jordan.

After he left Anand, Jordan gave himself a serious talking to. He'd turned into this boring, criticising excuse for a friend who no one wanted anything to do with. Martine didn't need his lectures. He wasn't yet sure what she did need. But Jordan knew that from now on he needed to let go of any dreams of having his mum home early. It *wasn't* going to happen. He had to stop counting the days and instead focus his attention on his friends, unless he wanted to find himself without any.

Maybe it would make these last eight days easier to get through. He remembered what his gran always told him when he couldn't wait for something to happen, like a birthday or a treat: *Time goes much faster when you don't watch the clock.*

And when you stop thinking about yourself and think about your friends instead, she might have added.

CHAPTER ELEVEN

The next day Jordan attempted to repair things with his friends. He started with Martine. 'Do you want to walk the dog with me after school? If you're not doing anything else.'

She'd been very cool towards him all day, so he was risking having his head bitten off, but she didn't turn him down flat, exactly. 'Can't,' she muttered.

'No, that's OK,' he was quick to reassure her.

'No, seriously, I can't. We've got to go for a trial run at the hairdresser's.'

Anand laughed in disbelief. 'You mean they, like, have to practise?'

Martine glowered at him. 'If they think I'm having

some curly girly effort, they'll have another battle on their hands. It's just not *fair*. Nobody would expect either of you to put up with this rubbish. It's just cos I'm a girl. It's like I have no choice. I'm sick of it all.'

'I bet you are,' Jordan sympathised. 'Look, forget it, we'll do it another day.'

'Excuse me! I can go,' Anand said, a little stung. 'If anybody cares.'

'I thought you'd be playing football,' Jordan said, surprised.

Anand looked over in the direction of the footie crew, who were paying him no attention at all. 'Football doesn't rule my life,' he said, dismissively.

Jordan was surprised to hear that, but he was pleased; one out of two wasn't a bad start.

Anand liked the idea of dogs, but he was always a little nervous of Jet. Today, as a special treat, Jordan let him hold the lead, and in no time Anand had overcome his nerves and was behaving as if the dog belonged to him, telling Jet off and tugging him back every time he tried to sniff around. In fact, Anand got a little over-eager and Jordan had to intervene.

'Be careful, man, you're going to choke the poor animal.'

The boys walked towards the river. It had been raining so much lately that the paths were very muddy and Anand said he wished he'd worn his old trainers; he knew he'd get it in the ear from his dad when he got home.

As they walked, Jordan tried to talk some more about Martine, and what the two of them could do to help her, but Anand didn't show much interest.

'Don't you even care?' Jordan asked impatiently.

'Not really,' Anand admitted. 'What's a bit of weight? Nobody died of it.'

'Well, no,' Jordan agreed. Obviously Martine wasn't that kind of fat. 'But if she keeps on eating like this all her life she might one day...'

'Yeah, yeah, yeah,' Anand cut him off. 'I mean...not any day soon.'

It wasn't like Anand to be so dismissive. Jordan could tell he had something else on his mind. 'Come on, what's up with you?' he asked him.

Anand hesitated but only for a moment. He wanted to get stuff off his chest, and when he did spill what it was, Jordan had to agree that Anand's troubles did seem more pressing than Martine's.

Some of it Jordan already knew; that the football boys had become bored with sweets and moved on to cigarettes, with all the extra risks this involved for Anand. They'd even started insisting on the best brands: 'Don't bring us any of that minging cheap rubbish.'

'Yeah, let's have some Marlboros or Silk Cut,' Connor Stewart told him, and the others had soon followed suit, putting in their own orders. But there had been a new development this week: now the boys were demanding money instead. That way, they said they could choose for themselves.

'Cut out the middle man,' Ricky Doherty had said, grinning.

'Don't worry, we'll spend the cash in your dad's shop,' Nutter Norris had assured him, 'so he'll still get the benefit.'

'Yeah, everyone's a winner,' the Biscuit had grinned.

Anand had tried to point out what was wrong with the logic of this arrangement, but as usual no one had listened to him. They seemed to assume the till was like an ever-open drawer and Anand could just dip in whenever he felt like it. Wasn't that the perk of living in a shop, they'd asked?

'Oh, God,' Jordan groaned. 'I told you, you should never have got involved in the first place. Just pull out, tell them you won't do it.'

'I can't,' Anand said miserably.

'Yes, you can.'

'I already tried,' he finally admitted. 'But they said they'll beat me up.'

'Don't be ridiculous,' Jordan told him. 'They haven't got a functioning brain between them, but even they wouldn't be that stupid.'

'You reckon?' Anand didn't look convinced.

'Think about it: what are they likely to do? Push you about a bit?'

Anand had already given the matter a lot of thought; he'd been lying in bed at night thinking about nothing else. He was actually relieved to be able to share his worst fears and lurid fantasies with Jordan. They might punch him, he suggested, kick him, maybe even *cut* him. He knew Ricky Doherty had a penknife. One of *his* favourite threats was, 'I'll make you even uglier, if that's possible.'

They might break his nose. Nutter Norris hadn't come by that nickname because of a fondness for peanuts. They might drag him to a secluded spot, tie him up and leave him there, where no one would find him until he starved to death...or was eaten by wild animals. They might tie him to the railway line.

Jordan couldn't help smiling at this one; Anand

definitely watched too many old movies in his opinion. His friend seemed to have covered most options, apart from burning and drowning, but Jordan wisely didn't point out these omissions.

'But the worst thing,' Anand summed up, then hesitated. 'No, the next to worst thing...' He could hardly bring himself to put it into words. 'They might spit on me.' Jordan suspected that what Anand felt about spitting amounted to a phobia. If anyone spat on him, Anand felt he would just...*die*.

Jordan wondered what on earth was left. 'So what's the worst thing?'

Anand looked completely crushed. 'They'd make me into a nobody,' he almost whispered.

Jordan knew what his friend meant. He'd seen them do this to other boys. They'd completely blank them, and make sure everyone else did too, until the boy felt almost as if he didn't exist – *was a nobody*. To Jordan it didn't sound the worst fate in the world, but he knew his friend well enough to realise that it would be to Anand.

'Listen, you've just got to stand up to them,' he urged, then quickly corrected himself. '*We've* got to stand up to them.'

But Anand shook his head. Even with Jordan's help this was clearly an impossibility for him.

151

'Then we've got to get help,' Jordan said, resignedly. 'You have to tell someone.'

'Oh, no. No way. You can't tell anyone. You've got to swear to me you won't tell a soul,' Anand looked close to tears.

Jordan hesitated. He knew he should be persuading Anand to report the bullying, even if most of it was still in his imagination. The boys had gone too far by making him steal from his own dad. But Jordan didn't want to desert his friend – he could see what a state he was in – so he reluctantly nodded.

'You swear?' Anand pressed him. 'On your mum's life?'

Jordan nodded again.

They walked on for a while but didn't talk much, and far from having built any bridges, when they parted Jordan felt an even bigger gulf between him and Anand. He thought of all the times in the past when one of his friends had been in some kind of a hole and he'd always known what to do, *how to fix it*, but now, when it really mattered, he couldn't seem to fix anything. He felt so useless – a total waste of space.

Jordan brooded over the business with Anand for the next couple of days. When he woke up each morning, it was now the first thing that went through his mind.

On Thursday, when his mum's wake-up call came, Jordan had to bite his tongue to resist the urge to confide in her.

'Good morning, sweetheart. How did you sleep?' she asked. 'Are you keeping that eczema under control?'

'Yes, Mum,' he told her for the umpteenth time.

'So what have you got on at school today?'

'Not much,' he sighed; it all seemed so trivial compared to his friend's troubles.

That evening, after another day of keeping it all to himself, Jordan was almost bursting to share the problem with someone. He really wished his dad would stay home for once; he didn't want to be on his own. But Kyle had weight training later, so his dad would take over at around 7.30 for a couple of hours. He had a short window of opportunity now if he wanted to take it.

Jordan and his dad were in the lounge, his dad dozing in front of the news. He woke with a huge yawn, which excited Jet, who leapt up from his prone position to hurl himself on top of him.

'All right, all right, nothing to get worked up about,' his dad said, fending off him. 'Nobody said the

W-A-L-K word.' Jet's tail started wagging even more manically, as if he knew how to spell.

'He knows what you're talking about,' Jordan complained.

His dad grabbed hold of the dog and held him between his legs while he did one of his favourite tricks, where he pulled the dog's mouth into different shapes so that it looked as if he were actually talking. 'What d'you think of it so far? Load of rubbish! Please, sir, can I have some more Bonios?'

Jordan shook his head. He was in no mood to be amused.

When his dad got down on the floor with Jet, and began wrestling with him, Jordan complained again. 'Da-a-ad, don't wind him up.'

'What's the matter with you?' his dad asked. 'You seem a bit down in the mouth.'

Jordan began, tentatively. 'Dad...'

'Yeah?'

'If someone asked you to keep a promise...'

'Yeah?'

'Would you keep it?'

'Probably,' his dad said. He'd stopped rolling on the floor and now sat with Jet between his knees, crossing and uncrossing his paws so that it looked as if the dog were dancing. Jordan found it even harder to get to the point.

'But what if...'

'What?'

'What if...'

His dad stopped playing and concentrated at last on the conversation. 'Oh, Jordan, for goodness' sake, spit it out.'

'What if you regretted ever saying you'd keep it?'

'Then I'd tell them. What's this about?'

Jordan shrugged. He couldn't break his promise to Anand. 'Nothing.'

'Honestly, I haven't got time for guessing games,' his dad said, getting up from the floor. 'If you want to come with me to see Mum for an hour or two we could continue this riveting conversation in the car.'

But Jordan shook his head. He knew he hadn't given his dad much to go on, but if his mum had been there she'd have already winkled it out of him, without Jordan actually having to break his promise. His dad was definitely no Sherlock Holmes, whereas his mum would have given Miss Marple a run for her money. And, what's more, she'd have told him what he had to do.

After his dad left, Jordan flicked through the TV

channels. He just caught the end of *The Simpsons*. The programme always made him think about Chrissie; it used to be her favourite. Jordan wished she were there right now.

The day that Chrissie moved out Jordan hadn't been too upset, because he'd felt sure she'd be home inside a week. In fact, just to wind her up, he'd said as she was leaving, 'Can I have your room, then?' because hers was bigger.

She'd been cross and asked him if he'd have been as quick to jump into her grave, and then when she realised what she'd said they'd both had hysterics.

Jordan knew that Chrissie partly blamed him for not arguing with their mum. If he'd begged her not to, Chrissie felt sure she would have listened. 'She doesn't care what I think, but if she thought you didn't want her to do it...'

But Jordan hadn't begged her. Kyle and his dad had made out it was going to be such a laugh with just the three of them – a 'Men Only' house for a change.

'Think of the freedom,' his dad had said. 'Think of the fun we'll have.'

Jordan was still waiting for the fun to start; there'd been no sign of it yet.

He was tempted to ring his sister now. He had

a good excuse: he needed some ideas about what to buy his mum for Christmas. But he'd be seeing Chrissie tomorrow; he could ask her then. Tonight she'd probably be out anyway with Chris, on his motorbike.

At least the thought of Christmas cheered him up. He'd got most of his presents, already wrapped, in the bottom of his wardrobe. He just wanted an extra one for his mum. He would ask Anand to come shopping with him on the weekend. No point asking Martine to come – it was the big day on Saturday – the *diabolical double wedding day*. Maybe by next week his friend would get her sanity back and stop bingeing on KitKats and Mars Bars.

Quite soon life would go back to normal for all of them. As soon as his mum came out, his gran and his sister would surely get over themselves and they'd all be a family again. Christmas was exactly what they all needed to blot out the past few months.

Jordan felt as if when his mum went underground his whole family had split down the middle and he had fallen into the hole. It was if he was waiting for someone to come along and dig him up, too. But now he had only five days more to wait, only one more weekend. He could survive that – just.

CHAPTER TWELVE

He was hanging from a metal track. It was some kind of railway line running on a narrow bridge across a deep gulf. He couldn't see if there was water at the bottom – it was too far away and too dark – but he could hear it rushing beneath him. He was hanging by his fingernails, in fear and danger of his life, yet all he could think of was how much he needed to take a leak.

He suddenly looked up to see Anand standing on the rails looking down at him, and not lifting a finger to help. Behind him were other faces he recognised – the footballers. They were encouraging Anand to spit on him, but instead his friend stepped forward and stood on his fingers.

Finally he lost his grip and was falling down and down and...

Jordan woke from one of those familiar dropping dreams where for a moment he felt as if he might fall out of the end of the bed. He couldn't think how, but he'd managed to miss his wake-up call from his mum, and so he was running late again. He dragged himself out of bed thinking that at least it was Friday.

By the skin of his teeth he managed to get into school on time, but that didn't save him from another lecture later in the day from his form tutor. Mrs Raynsworth met Jordan in the corridor and reminded him – he had genuinely managed to forget – that on Monday she was meeting his father to follow up the far-from-positive report she'd given him on Jordan in October.

'And I'm afraid I shall have to tell him how little improvement there's been since. Rather the opposite: things seem to be getting worse, don't they, Jordan?' She waited for a response from Jordan, but none was forthcoming. 'Almost every subject teacher I've spoken

same story to tell. It makes me very sad
she finished.

an briefly felt sad too, on his teacher's behalf;
as beyond feeling sad on his own. In the past he
ght have given her the smile, but Mrs Raynsworth,
like everyone else, had become immune to Jordan's
smile. And, anyway, he couldn't just turn it on like
that; he had to have something to smile about, and
there was precious little at the moment.

Double art, however, was one of the few lessons
Jordan still found worth going to. They were working
on a cushion cover project with their teacher, Mrs
Hardy. They'd researched Celtic designs and then,
using batik and tie dye, transferred them to pieces of
fabric. They were finally making up the patterned
fabric into cushion covers, which they could take
home and use as Christmas presents.

Anand had sneered at the idea, but Jordan, unusually
for him these days, had felt positive about the whole
project. He intended to give his mum the cushion for
Christmas. In fact, he'd even found time to decorate
some extra fabric, which he'd persuaded Mrs Hardy to
let him make into a hot-water bottle cover. He thought
it would be something she would really appreciate when
she came out into winter temperatures.

Today was their last art lesson before they broke up and a lot of people were still working on the first stages of the project – largely because they'd spent the previous lessons dossing about, or time-wasting with rubber-band fights, or dripping hot wax onto each others' hands. Now Mrs Hardy was trying to help some of them cram four weeks' work into one lesson.

Jordan was busily employed at the sewing machine, sewing together the pieces of his hot-water bottle cover and edging it with tape. He was fondly imagining the smile on his mum's face when he gave it to her.

Anand suddenly appeared at his elbow. 'You look pleased with yourself,' he told Jordan, thrusting two pieces of still-damp fabric in front of him. 'Do mine for me, will you?'

'Do it yourself,' Jordan told him.

Anand wore a *pretty-please* expression, which was actually far from pretty. Jordan groaned and snatched the fabric from his friend. 'But you owe me,' he said. 'Christmas shopping tomorrow, in town, OK?'

'Yeah, whatever,' Anand would have agreed to anything rather than have to sit and sew *like a girl*. Of course, he knew better than to voice that opinion in front of Martine. She'd have done something unspeakable to Anand and his cushion cover. But there was no way he'd be giving it to his mum for Christmas. He'd never hear the end of it from his dad, who was an even bigger chauvinist than Anand.

Martine had been in a bad mood all day – with the impending wedding – so neither of the boys had dared say two words to her. At the end of school the three of them stood together in awkward silence.

'Hope it's...erm...soon over,' was Jordan's best effort.

'Yeah, see you Monday – if you survive,' Anand added less tactfully.

'Part of me hopes I don't,' Martine admitted.

Jordan watched his friend walk off, like a condemned woman heading down death row. He, for a change, was looking forward to his weekend: shopping tomorrow with Anand, then fishing on Sunday...and after that he really would be on the last lap.

After school Jordan went home to collect Jet before heading off to see his mum. It had been a couple of weeks since he'd taken the dog to visit her. Jet didn't know Jordan's mum, of course, but he still got very excited and scrabbled around the top of the pipe, as if left to his own devices he'd like to dig her up. Jordan was very tempted to let him.

As soon as he arrived, his aunt put up the closed sign and turned away the few people waiting to talk to his mum.

'Let the boy have a bit of privacy,' she told them, bossily. 'It's his mum down there, you know. He's had to manage without her for five months.'

Jordan wished yet again that the ground would open up and swallow him, too.

'So, what's new?' his mum asked.

Jordan shrugged. 'Nothing, as usual,' he said. 'I can't wait for Christmas.'

'Well, it'll soon be here.'

'It doesn't feel like it. It's not a bit Christmassy at home,' he grumbled. 'We've got no decorations up.'

'I have,' his mum told him.

'Oh, very funny,' Jordan said.

'No, I have. Someone brought me a tiny tree with a few silver balls on it. They brought me some lights as well, but they kept flashing and gave me a headache, so I told them to take them away again.'

'When are you going to buy your presents?' Jordan asked.

'Give me a chance. I'm not out yet.'

'I've got most of mine,' Jordan bragged.

'What've you got me? Give us a clue!'

'Not on your life,' Jordan laughed. He knew his mum better than that. She always tried to wheedle surprises out of you and she was too good at it. 'All I'm telling you is it's something you'll really want when you come out.'

'Sunglasses?' she guessed.

'Not even close.'

'It's not a wheelchair, is it?'

'Why?' he asked, alarmed.

'I was joking. I probably won't be able to walk for a day or two, that's all, just until I get my legs working again. But for goodness' sake don't start worrying about that now,' she told him.

'How'll you cook the Christmas dinner in a wheelchair?'

'Lots of people do,' she reminded him. 'Anyway, I shall probably sit in the corner, wearing sunglasses and a fur coat, and give everyone else orders. It'll be fine. It'll be the best Christmas ever.'

Yeah, Jordan couldn't argue with that. He wouldn't care what jobs he was given if it meant that life would get back to normal.

Only five days – you could count those on one hand!

*

When Jordan got home he was surprised to hear voices coming from the lounge. It was early for his dad to be home. He recognised his brother's voice and his dad's, but there was a third he didn't know. Jordan was even more surprised when he saw that the voice belonged to that creep of a reporter, the one Kyle had had a fight with. You'd never have guessed it to see them now, sitting together on the sofa, perfectly cosy. Jordan wondered what was going on.

'You remember Mr Starr,' his dad said, introducing Jordan.

The reporter smiled, but Jordan didn't return the smile. He did remember Mr Starr, but it was nothing to smile about. For a few moments he hung around expecting someone to explain what he was doing there, but the conversation seemed to have come to an abrupt end.

There was an official-looking letter on the table and Jordan saw it had *The Guinness Book of Records* logo on it. His dad nodded: 'It's definite,' he said. 'It's been dropped.'

Jordan felt confused. Everyone already knew that; they were all getting their heads round the fact. Why was it making his dad look so odd? And why was the reporter there? An awkward silence followed and

Jordan began to feel as if he was in the way.

'Aren't you going to be late for Gran?' Kyle asked.

Jordan looked at the clock; it was nearly five. He nodded and left, still no wiser. Apart from his initial dislike of the reporter, Jordan had no reason to feel so uneasy, but he did. He felt as if there was a bad smell in the air and this time it wasn't Jet who was responsible.

He decided that the most likely reason for the reporter's visit was in connection with his mum's digging-out party. No doubt he wanted to mastermind the entire celebrations and get his newspaper a ringside seat. Jordan hated the idea that next Tuesday, when his mum would finally come out, his very first sight of her would be under the glare of cameras, surrounded by hordes of strangers. He'd have liked a small family celebration, but that was never going to happen.

When Jordan suggested it, his dad had said, 'Don't be daft, lad. She'll want all the bells and whistles, the fireworks, the cameras. That's why she did it in the first place: so everyone would take notice.'

Of course, Jordan thought, his mum would want the whole wide world there. Seeing him again would be a small treat in comparison.

'You look like someone coming to the end of a long prison sentence,' his gran told him when he got there.

But Jordan shook his head. 'Don't want to talk about it any more. I'm *bored* with it all.' And he was – *bored* out of his skull, *bored* beyond endurance. He quickly changed the subject. 'Mmmm, something smells good.' At least he could enjoy his gran's lasagne – hers wouldn't still be frozen in the middle.

He went through to the lounge and found his sister in exactly the same position as before, curled up on the sofa, still poring over holiday magazines, as if she hadn't moved since his previous visit.

'Haven't you decided yet?' he asked her.

Chrissie sighed. 'Everything's so expensive. I think we're just going to have to wait and get one of those last-minute bookings. Go in next week and see what they've got.'

'Why, when are you going?' Jordan asked with a look of horror on his face. He'd stupidly assumed this was a summer holiday they were planning.

'Wednesday? Thursday? As soon as we finish work.'

'But what about Christmas?' he asked.

'What about it?' she laughed. 'Nobody cancelled it, did they?'

Jordan thought for a terrible moment he might burst into tears. He struggled to get himself under control. 'Why would you want to go away at Christmas?' he asked more reasonably.

'Sun, sea, peace and quiet – d'you need any more reasons?' Chrissie asked. Then, seeing Jordan's expression, she softened a little. 'It's not like we'd all be together, is it?'

'Why not?' he demanded.

'You know why not.'

'But it'll all be over by then.'

Chrissie rolled her eyes as if she had her doubts about that.

Jordan tried a different approach. 'What about Gran?'

'What about me?' she asked, coming in just then.

'We were talking about Christmas,' Chrissie told her, rolling her eyes again.

'Oh, that,' his gran said dismissively. 'Let's not spoil our meal thinking about *that*.' The emphasis she put on the word let Jordan know the conversation was over.

As they ate, the bubbling, delicious golden food seemed to turn to sand in Jordan's mouth. He kept quiet for much of the time, but in the end he couldn't help himself. 'According to Anand's dad it'll all be chaos, strikes and terrorist attacks. He says you'd have to be stark staring bananas to want to fly over the holidays. Apart from all these planes that bits keep falling off.'

'My word, you're very cheerful tonight,' his gran observed.

'A regular bundle of laughs,' Chrissie agreed.

When Jordan got home he had the house to himself for a while, which gave him the chance to get his head round this new disappointment. Later, when his dad came in, he seemed quiet and distracted too, and Jordan decided now was not a good time to tell him Chrissie's plans.

Neither did his dad seem in the best mood to be approached for extra pocket money, but this weekend was Jordan's final chance to get his mum's last present, so it couldn't wait.

'I thought you'd got all yours,' his dad remarked.

'I need an extra one for Mum. I'll pay you back when I get my Christmas money,' he promised.

'What makes you so sure you're going to get any?' his dad asked, a slight smile on his face.

'I always get *some*,' Jordan argued.

'How much?'

'Five pounds?'

Amazingly, his dad coughed up without another word. It had proved so easy that afterwards Jordan thought what an idiot he'd been – not asking for more.

CHAPTER THIRTEEN

Jordan and Anand walked into Highcross Shopping Centre. The only shopping they were planning was Jordan's; Anand had no money, as usual. Jordan had had to pay his friend's bus fare.

'Even if I had any, I wouldn't be spending it on my minging family,' Anand told Jordan. He was especially angry today with his dad for embarrassing him in front of his friend.

When Jordan had called to pick up Anand, Mr Solanki had been in a very serious mood. Without any initial pleasantries, he'd looked Jordan straight in the eye and asked, 'Tell me, Jordan, do you, by any possibility, smoke?'

Fortunately Jordan had no difficulty returning Mr Solanki's stare. Whatever games Anand was up to, it was nothing to do with him. Jordan didn't smoke, he didn't ever intend to, and he told Anand's dad that. 'I think it's a mug's game, to be honest.'

He wasn't sure whether Mr Solanki believed him or whether it had helped his friend. But it was clear his dad was onto Anand, even if he couldn't prove anything yet.

'You really are going to have to watch your back,' Jordan warned Anand. But he refused to talk about it.

Anand didn't mind coming along for the ride, but he couldn't understand why Jordan wanted to get his mum another present. 'You already made her one,' he pointed out.

Jordan had made two, in fact, but he didn't count those, although he knew his mum would. He wanted to spend his money on her, too. He wanted her to know how much he'd missed her and how glad he was to have her back.

Jordan was feeling better than he had in weeks. Town was full of Christmas shoppers with lists in their hands and he suddenly felt like everyone else for a change. Next Friday, which was Christmas Day, his life would be the same as everyone else's at last. They'd all be together – a proper family again.

Jordan dragged Anand round Boots for hours, trying out perfumes until they both absolutely stank, but everything he liked proved too expensive.

He knew it was time to go home when Anand started getting bored – always a dangerous situation. Jordan quickly bought a photo frame and a tea towel. A tea towel wasn't the most exciting present, but it had a cheesy poem on it about mothers. Anand wasn't impressed. 'Pass the sick bucket,' he told Jordan, but Jordan didn't care. He knew his mum would appreciate it.

The two boys were heading back to the bus station as they saw their bus just pulling away. They settled down for a short wait. Quite a queue had formed behind them when Anand said, 'Uh-oh. Here come the bad boys.'

Jason Carlisle, Nutter Norris and Connor Stewart joined the queue, and Anand gave them a friendly nod. It really annoyed Jordan that he could still pretend to be friends with them when they'd been so rotten to him. Jordan kept his back turned, but he could hear the boys laughing and swearing, and he felt sure he heard his name mentioned.

He wanted to keep his distance from the boys, but when the bus arrived Anand immediately started up the stairs, and Jordan knew the others would follow. At least Anand chose the front seat; Jordan hoped the others would sit at the back. But it was a forlorn hope. They crowded in right behind, all three slapping them round the backs of their heads by way of greeting.

'Let's see what you got,' Connor ordered, but Jordan ignored him.

'S'just Christmas presents,' Anand explained. 'For his mum.'

'Didn't know Santa delivered down drainpipes,' Jason joked.

'Imagine looking up and seeing that fat backside coming towards you,' Nutter Norris guffawed.

'His mum's going to be out for Christmas,' Anand told them cheerfully. 'She's only got four days left.'

Jordan wished his friend would shut up and not give the boys any more encouragement.

'They letting her out for good behaviour?' Connor asked. 'You never know, she might be one of those who can't hack it on the outside.'

'Yeah, blubbing and begging to go back down,' Nutter Norris laughed.

Jason Carlisle burst into song: 'I am a mole and I live in a HOLE!'

All the boys seemed to find this genuinely funny and original. For Jordan, the jokes were all so old now they almost had mould growing on them. It exasperated him to see Anand laughing too. He wanted to shake some sense into his friend, but he kept on looking forward, hoping that the boys would get bored with the subject, which they finally did. Although he wasn't a lot happier with the new topic.

'Why don't you play footie any more, Gibbons?' Connor asked him.

'I'm always asking him, aren't I?' Anand joined in, but Connor cut him off.

'No one's talking to you, Skanki.'

'Been busy,' Jordan mumbled, immediately realising his mistake.

'Visiting the undead?' Jason joked.

Jordan ignored this.

'You should come down – tomorrow,' Connor said. It was clearly an order.

'Can't,' Jordan mumbled.

'He goes fishing,' Anand explained. Jordan gritted his teeth. Why couldn't Anand just shut up? He wished the bus would get a move on instead of stopping so often. He wanted to get off and escape from these idiots.

'I'll play tomorrow,' Anand offered.

Connor gripped the back of Anand's neck. 'I'm talking to the ventriloquist,' he said nastily, 'not the dummy.'

Even now Anand didn't have the sense to keep quiet. 'I'll bring some stuff,' he squeaked.

'We don't want *stuff*,' Connor told him, leaning forward and whispering, 'you know what we want.'

The other two boys flicked Anand's ears, lightly, almost playfully, but Jordan could see they meant to hurt him.

Jordan finally spun round and said, 'Leave him alone.'

At last they'd got a reaction out of him. 'Oh, the zombie can talk,' Jason said in mock fear.

'We haven't done anything to him...y*et*,' Connor Stewart said, menacingly.

'You mean apart from blackmailing him,' Jordan finally confronted them.

The boys burst out laughing as if this were a gross exaggeration.

'*Blackmailing him?*' Connor said with scorn. 'Our mate Skanki?'

All the boys looked at Anand, who shrugged and shook his head as if he had no idea what Jordan could possibly be talking about. Jordan was way past being angry with him.

'But even if we were,' Connor said, 'who you gonna tell – *your mum*?'

'She gonna rise out of her grave,' Jason laughed, waving his arms about like a ghost, 'and come and haunt us?'

'Must be awful lonely down there...under the ground,' Connor went on, 'all on her own... Maybe we should go and...visit her?'

Jordan had to get away from them before he completely lost it. They were only halfway home, but he got out of his seat and raced to get off the bus.

'Where you going?' Anand called, but Jordan didn't even turn to answer.

He jumped before the bus had properly stopped and staggered forward several steps before he caught his balance. He kept on walking fast until he got tired and slackened his pace. It was getting dark and he didn't fancy the walk home, but at least it was all on well-lit main roads.

He kept telling himself he'd over-reacted; those idiots were only doing what they'd done ever since his mum was first buried – trying to find ways to wind him up. But this time it had reminded him too much of another occasion. Not that they would have known about it – nobody outside his family knew; he hadn't even told Anand and Martine. They'd been warned by the police not to tell anyone in case some other stupid idiot – exactly like those stupid idiots on the bus – decided to copy the idea.

Three months after his mum had been buried, his dad had got a call from her in the middle of the night. She'd been almost hysterical. Someone had rung her, on her mobile, and threatened to pour petrol down the pipe and set light to it. She'd pressed the emergency alarm to wake his uncle and then called his dad. The police had been there in minutes. They'd taken it very seriously and they'd caught the person in no time.

It had turned out to be someone his mum used to work with, called Dave Moon. He told the police he'd been on the night shift at the factory where he worked – and just got bored. He'd rung her from the factory-floor phone, hadn't even had the intelligence to withhold the number, so it hadn't taken the police long to track him down.

'It were only a prank,' he swore, 'that's all. I'd never have done it. We were mates. It were just for a laugh.'

He wasn't laughing much after he'd spent a night in a police cell – and then lost his job as a result.

Jordan hadn't known anything about it until later the next day, after the man had been released by the police. His mum had seemed to get over it amazingly quickly, once she knew who it was. But it was after that that Jordan's dreams had got much worse, once he'd realised how very vulnerable she was, down there alone.

Jordan stamped along now, his shopping banging against his legs, his hood up against the cold. Although he wasn't on his own like his mum was, under the ground, sometimes he felt so alone he might as well have been. So it was a big relief when he reached the next bus stop to see his friend waiting for him.

'You owe me, mate,' Anand told Jordan. 'I hope you're planning a mint present for me.'

In your dreams, Jordan thought, but he didn't tell Anand that. Part of him wanted to ask if the boys had said – or done – anything to make Anand get off the bus. But he preferred just to believe that Anand had at last realised who his friends really were.

As they got nearer to home they passed the end of the drive up to the golf club – the venue for the diabolical double wedding. Both weddings would probably be over, but Martine's family would be celebrating at the joint party. From the road the boys could see one or two people in wedding gear standing outside the building, smoking.

They didn't have to discuss the idea between them; it seemed to occur to them simultaneously. They set off across the grass, grinning. It was pretty dark, and if they kept off the drive no one would see them sneaking round the building. They peered in through each window they passed until they located the party suite. There was no mistaking it: a lot of very loud country and western music was bouncing off the walls and people were almost yelling in an attempt to hold conversations over the top of it. The boys rested their noses on the window ledge and scanned the room, looking for Martine.

It took a few moments but Jordan spotted her first and nudged Anand. He pointed to a far corner, where their friend was almost unrecognisable in a pink frothy outfit only slightly less extravagant than her sister, Shelly's, who was sitting nearby. Martine was at another table with a couple of young cousins, half-heartedly picking at a plate of food. It made the two boys hungry just to see the huge buffet piled high with delicacies, including big bowls of dessert. Clearly the food police had gone off duty now the weddings were over.

As they watched, Stu, Martine's new step-dad, came over to her carrying a bowl of what looked like trifle. He was holding it out like a peace offering, but Martine wasn't easily bought. He was clearly trying hard to get a smile out of her. When Martine gave Stu that familiar scorching look, the boys had some sympathy with him. They'd both been on the receiving end of that look lots of times. But Stu was in too good a mood – or too merry – to be deflated, and he sat down next to her, attempting once more to cheer her up.

Martine got up from the table and stalked across the room, trying to look as dignified as she could in a dress that made her resemble a trifle herself. Suddenly she must have hit a slippery patch on the floor, because she slid quite a distance before ending up almost doing the splits. Jordan and Anand let out a gasp, but in a fraction of a second Martine was back on her feet. They'd never seen her move so fast. She glanced around, checking that no one had witnessed her humiliation, before she carried on, holding her dress together, looking as haughty as ever.

The two boys had to drop to the ground and stuff

their hands into their mouths to prevent discovery. They sat on the ground, rocking with laughter. They knew that they could never reveal what they had just seen to Martine, not if they hoped to keep her friendship. They immediately took a solemn oath to that effect.

'She'd kill us,' Jordan told Anand simply.

Anand agreed. 'It'd be more than our lives are worth. But it's a pity, all the same,' he grinned. How he would have loved to be able to use that little piece of ammunition!

CHAPTER FOURTEEN

The next day, while the early morning mist was still hanging in the air, Jordan was already by the river, before any other fishermen arrived. He carefully set up his swim: his seat, his rod and rest, his landing net and bait trays. There was no need for him to rush; it was still too early to catch anything. At this time of year even the fish seemed to like a lie-in.

Before settling down to watch his line, Jordan followed his grandad's infallible remedy for cold hands. Kneeling by the edge, he plunged his fists into the ice-cold water and held them there until they were almost numb. It was an extreme measure, but it never failed. The pain lasted a few minutes, but now at least he wouldn't be plagued by frozen fingers all morning.

The sky was a pinky grey, no clouds, just ribbons of mist; the silence so sweet Jordan could almost taste it. Across the fields he could see the first sign of the sun as it began the slow job of burning off the mist, which would probably take at least the next couple of hours.

Jordan watched a heron eyeballing him from the other bank. They were so common along here, and so used to people, it was only when you were almost upon them that they deigned to open their prehistoric wings and skim silently over the river. They always seemed to Jordan the height of cool.

Long before he expected to get a bite, his float bobbed down. Jordan jumped to his feet and tensed his line. He gave it a tug, waited a second then reeled in fast, his line whistling. He could tell it was a good-sized fish, maybe a personal best. He could feel the adrenalin pumping as he successfully drew the fish in closer until it was near enough to net.

As the excitement cooled, Jordan felt the familiar pang of disappointment that his grandpa wasn't there to witness his catch. No matter what size fish Jordan landed, his grandpa always said the same: 'Call that a catch? I've used bigger fish as bait. Now, *this* is a fish.' And he'd reach into his keep net and lift out a monster that made Jordan's catch look like a tadpole. Then his grandpa would laugh so much at his own joke that Jordan would have to join in.

It seemed to Jordan that his grandpa could actually tell what the fish were thinking, sometimes even before the fish itself had thought it. On a slow morning neither of them might catch a thing for an hour or two, but then his grandpa would turn to Jordan and say, 'OK. Now I'm going to catch one.' And he usually did. His grandpa said he was a great believer in sending out positive messages.

Jordan examined the fish he'd caught now. Despite the struggle it had put up the fish wasn't enormous, but respectable. Jordan had no scales to weigh it, but after he'd tenderly dislodged the hook he let the fish rest on his hands, trying to *guesstimate* its weight: four, maybe five pounds. A chubb was easy to recognise by its big, wide mouth, silver colouring and the slimy feel of its skin. Jordan could identify most of the fish in this stretch of river: as well as chubb, at some point he and his grandpa had caught roach, bream, perch, and, on odd occasions, a large carp or barbell.

After this initial activity, things went very quiet. Jordan had a few nibbles but no real action. Slowly other fishermen arrived and set up their own swims, but after a friendly nod Jordan spoke to no one, not even his grandpa's mate Stan, who chose the peg beside him. He was happy to be off inside his own head, just thinking about the next catch and watching his float for the slightest tremor. His dad was cooking a rare Sunday roast dinner that Jordan was already looking forward to, and he'd told him to be home for one o'clock, which only gave him the morning to fish.

So Jordan was far from thrilled when he saw Anand coming around the curve of the path, and even less thrilled to see that he was running away from three or four other boys still in the distance. Jordan didn't even have to guess who they were.

He groaned and got to his feet, reeling in his line as fast as he could. He'd brought one of his best rods and his first concern was to keep it safe. He quickly dismantled it and carried it over to Stanley.

'Will you keep an eye on this? And watch my gear? I won't be long.' He glanced over his shoulder towards the boys closing in on Anand. Stan nodded and grunted; he had clearly seen the reason for Jordan's request.

There was a loud whining noise as two boys on mopeds joined the chase. Jordan knew the noise would infuriate the fishermen. He would have liked to tell them they were no friends of his, but there wasn't time. He ran towards Anand to head him off. He took his friend's arm, pulling him away from the path, towards a small area of rough ground that led to some allotments. If the boys were planning to get heavy with Anand, Jordan didn't want them too close to the water with the added temptation of pushing him in. But Anand was panting so much he soon had to stop.

'What on earth's going on?' Jordan asked, but Anand was too breathless to answer. In a moment the boys had surrounded them. The mopeds stopped and Ricky Doherty and Connor Stewart jumped off the backs and took charge.

Jordan opened his mouth to speak but Ricky Doherty barked, 'First off, you keep out of this.'

'Unless you like the taste of hospital food,' Connor Stewart warned him.

Jordan had always suspected that both boys were mostly big talkers, what his grandma called *all mouth and no trousers*. But today, with so many others to back them up, Jordan wasn't about to test this theory.

The boys riding the mopeds kept revving their engines and creating a stream of petrol fumes, as well as deafening them all. Jordan could see some of the fishermen already scowling at them. Over the noise, Connor Stewart was shouting at Anand, 'Don't say you weren't warned, Skanki.'

'Look,' Anand tried to explain, 'I'll get some...tomorrow.' But tomorrow wasn't soon enough for them.

Despite all the football they played, the boys were struggling to get their breath back after having to chase Anand so far. Ricky and Connor, who hadn't had to run, told Anand in a variety of colourful language to keep his mouth shut – if he wanted to keep his teeth. Jordan didn't seriously believe the boys would try to beat them up in full view of the fishermen and decided to call their bluff.

'Come on, let's get out of here,' he told Anand, grabbing him by the arm. But the other boys blocked their path and pushed them roughly back into line. Clearly, it wasn't going to be quite that easy.

'I told you, stay out of this,' Ricky reminded him.

'Unless you want your mum buried – for real this time,' Connor Stewart added.

Now they were really being idiotic. Jordan found himself laughing. He turned to go again, but Nutter Norris caught hold of him and pulled him back as if he were on a piece of elastic.

'OK, now you get to choose,' Ricky told Anand. 'Come with us, settle your debts and get to play football...'

'...or hang out with this loser, grave-digger boy, and never play again,' Connor closed the offer.

For a moment, Jordan watched as his friend looked like he was seriously considering the choice. He really began to wonder why he bothered with Anand. It felt like the absolute final straw. But then his friend surprised him by grinning at Jordan and saying, 'Let's go. I never was much good at football.'

'You said it,' Jason Carlisle agreed.

'You're going to regret this,' Ricky warned him.

'Oh, and what are you going to do about it?' Jordan asked him, wearily. Connor and Ricky glanced over their shoulders. They obviously couldn't do much here and now, with all the fishermen looking on, but they wouldn't let these two off that easily.

'Chuck 'em in the nettles,' Connor ordered the others. Jordan and Anand found themselves manhandled into a nettle patch. Finally even Anand could see the funny side of things: it was December, after all, and the nettles were pretty well dead. Compared to his lurid fantasies this punishment seemed completely pathetic. He lay on his back, giggling, and when Jordan joined in it only served to wind the bullies up further. Ricky kicked them a few times, then Connor Stewart bent down and yanked off one of Anand's trainers.

'Let's give them something to really laugh about,' he shouted. He turned and lobbed the trainer into the river. The other boys joined in, whooping with pleasure as they stripped Jordan of his trainers too.

The resulting splashes caused an uproar of complaint from the fishermen, to which the boys responded with aggressive V-signs, then Ricky Doherty and Connor Stewart jumped back onto the mopeds and headed off down the path. The others followed as fast as they could, leaving Jordan and Anand still lying on the ground, laughing.

'Oh, man, I am going to be in deep you-know-what with my dad,' Anand groaned, not laughing any more. 'Those were nearly new trainers.'

'Oh, give up moaning,' Jordan told him, getting to his feet. 'Come on. Let's go and get them back.'

'How're we gonna do that?' Anand asked, pulling himself up.

'We're going fishing,' said Jordan.

It took a quarter of an hour's fishing for Jordan to hook all four trainers, reeling them in painfully slowly, afraid they might slip off the hook at the last moment. He had to grab hold of Anand when he tried to help by reaching too far out and almost joined the trainers in the river. Some of the fishermen looked on, shaking their heads and grinning, but thankfully they kept their opinions to themselves.

After they'd emptied out the weeds and other rubbish, not to mention the smelly river water, the trainers looked and smelled pretty gross.

'Aw, man, they *stink*,' Anand groaned.

But the smell was nothing compared to the discomfort of forcing their feet into the sodden footwear and then squelching their way back down the canal path.

'At least you've got them back,' Jordan pointed out.

But Anand wasn't exactly bursting with gratitude. 'My dad's gonna skin me alive,' he moaned.

Jordan didn't bother arguing the point. Anand's dad, although he could be friendly, even charming to his customers, was a tyrant at home compared to Jordan's own father. Even so, as he approached his house, Jordan wasn't looking forward to telling his dad what had happened to his shoes either. He tried to come up with one of his famous implausible excuses, but he couldn't for the moment think of anything more incredible than what had actually happened.

He crept in the back door in his socks, leaving the disgusting trainers outside on the step to dry off, hoping no one would know what had happened.

Jordan was immediately cheered up by the rather good smell that greeted him when he entered the house.

'Just in time,' his dad said. 'Wash your hands and come and sit down.'

His dad looked bright pink and breathless, and there were beads of sweat on his forehead. The kitchen was in a complete state of chaos and Jordan thought it looked as if his dad had used every pan in the house.

He washed his hands and went to the table. The food was already plated up and his dad had put a huge helping of chicken and stuffing and roast potatoes and vegetables in front of him. There was even gravy – a bit thin and watery, but quite an achievement for his dad. Jordan hadn't eaten like this at home for a long time. He suspected his dad might be trying to get in some practice for the following week, when his mum came home.

Just the thought of his mum back in her empty place at the table made Jordan stop for a moment. His whole body relaxed and he closed his eyes so that he could imagine it better. When he opened them he found his dad and Kyle looking at him, oddly. Perhaps they thought Jordan had suddenly found religion and was privately saying grace. Jordan just grinned at them, then grabbed his knife and fork and started to tuck into his food.

'So, d'you catch anything?' his dad asked.

Jordan shrugged. 'Not much biting; too cold.'

'I don't know why you bother at this time of year,' Kyle said, between mouthfuls. 'All you do is get wet and smelly.'

'Speaking of which...' his dad said, noticing for the first time that Jordan hadn't changed out of his fishing gear.

Jordan grinned again, then tried to steer his dad away from the subject. 'Hmm, good grub, Dad. Nearly as good as Mum's.' His dad smiled, still looking distinctly red from his efforts. 'We could have this with Mum on Tuesday.'

Jordan caught a look between his dad and his brother and stopped eating, the fork halfway to his mouth. He imagined the look was something to do with the celebrations. Of course, they'd probably go on until late in the evening. They wouldn't get time alone with his mum before the following morning. Jordan sighed. 'Well, maybe Wednesday then.'

He was about to start eating again, but noticed that Kyle and his dad had stopped now. His dad put down his cutlery and took a drink. He suddenly looked really uncomfortable.

'You've got to tell him, Dad,' Kyle said.

'Let's get dinner eaten first,' his dad bargained.

But Kyle pressed him. 'Get it over with.'

Now Jordan was worried. He could tell by the look on his dad's face that something definitely wasn't right.

'There's been a change of plan, Jordan.'

But he couldn't hear any more. He had a sick feeling in his stomach and he quickly pushed his chair back from the table. He headed for the bathroom, feeling as if he might bring back all the delicious food he'd just tucked away.

'Jordie, come back!' his dad called after him. 'Don't be like that, lad.'

But Jordan was deaf to his dad's calls. He locked the bathroom door and sat on the side of the bath concentrating on not being sick. He could hear his dad outside the door, trying the handle. He sat there taking deep breaths, trying to stop the buzzing that was going on inside his head. His dad was talking but Jordan wouldn't listen. It was bad news, that much he knew, and he didn't want to hear it.

Jordan slid down until he was sitting on the floor, his back against the bath. He hugged his knees against his chest. He was in no hurry to come out. He would stay in there all day if he had to.

CHAPTER FIFTEEN

Jordan could hear that his dad was still outside the door. All the lovely food must by now have gone to waste, but Jordan didn't care about that.

'Come out and talk about it, Jordan, please,' his dad begged.

Jordan went on ignoring his dad for as long as he could, for what felt like hours, but eventually he realised that he couldn't stay in the bathroom indefinitely. He was cold and bored and he'd run so many different scenarios through his head he began to wonder if the real story could be any worse than what he'd been imagining.

When he finally opened the door, Jordan made

sure his dad knew that he may have relented, but he couldn't be got round easily. He pushed his dad's arm roughly away. 'So...' he asked, angrily, 'what's going on?'

'Your mum's going to stop down a little bit longer...' his dad began.

That much Jordan had guessed.

'It'll only be another week or so,' Kyle added.

'Until the new year,' his dad finished off. 'But, listen, when you hear why, I promise you, Jordie, you'll agree it's going to be worth it.'

Jordan had a drumming noise in his ears that made it hard to concentrate on what his dad was saying. So afterwards he had only a sketchy idea, but the gist of it was that the slimy reporter, the one that had been at their house on Friday, had offered his mum a thousand pounds a day to stay down until New Year's Eve – actually coming out on the stroke of midnight – and giving his paper exclusive rights to the story and photos.

'That's ten thousand pounds,' Kyle pointed out. 'Think of all the things that'll buy.'

He and his dad seemed to expect Jordan to jump in the air with delight at the prospect of a trip to Disney World or a holiday at CenterParcs. Of course, at any other time, Jordan probably would have done, but not now.

'Or we could go somewhere hot and sunny where there's good fishing,' his dad suggested. 'Thailand or Mexico – you can choose.'

They both kept offering more reasons why this was really good news, but not one of them impressed Jordan.

'The thing is,' Kyle told him, 'it'll make her record so much more solid. No one's going to come along and easily break it once she's been down a hundred and *sixty* days. It'll be golden. It'll stand for ever.'

Jordan still hadn't said anything. He just waited until the two of them ran out of reasons why it was the best thing since sliced bread, then he got up and went off to his room. He stayed there for the rest of the day, and later, when his mum rang his mobile, he ignored it. He ignored it three times.

Later still, when his dad brought in the landline, he hid under his quilt, pretending to be asleep, even though it was only nine o'clock.

As his dad walked back downstairs Jordan could hear him saying, 'Don't worry, duck, he'll come round, once he's slept on it.'

Jordan was so choked up he again found himself on

the verge of crying, but this time with anger and frustration. He knew exactly what everyone else would tell him: 'It's been nearly a hundred and fifty days already, what's ten more?' But Jordan began to feel as if he were in some kind of horrible nightmare with any prospect of ever seeing his mum again receding into the far distance, on and on into infinity.

He was furious with his dad and his brother. They'd obviously known since Friday, ever since the slimy reporter's visit, and they'd kept it from him, until it was all signed and sealed. They must have discussed it with his mum and agreed the deal between them, without anyone bothering to ask him. Now he could see that the roast dinner had been to soften him up, to get round him before they broke the news. It made him feel even more sick and manipulated.

Jordan hated that reporter and wished Kyle had given him a real pasting. If he hadn't come sneaking round with his wads of money his mum would have been coming out in *two days' time*! Not only would he have to wait an extra ten days, but what kind of lousy Christmas would they have now, all crowded round a stupid drainpipe opening their presents? Well, he wouldn't go up there on Christmas Day; they couldn't make him. He'd go to his gran's instead.

Jordan was desperate to share his bad news with someone. It was too awful to keep to himself. He searched for his phone to ring his friends. He started with Anand, who took ages to answer.

When Anand finally came on he told Jordan, 'Can't talk. I'm in up to my neck now.' He seemed to be whispering, his hand muffling the phone so that Jordan could only barely hear what he was saying. 'I told you my dad'd go crazy about my trainers.'

'He'll get over it,' Jordan replied. As if a pair of muddy trainers was the crime of the century.

'Yeah, well, now he's definitely missed the ciggies. He's got it into his head it was *me*.' Anand sounded quite indignant.

'It *was* you,' Jordan pointed out.

But Anand ignored the reality check. 'Anyway, gotta go. Gotta lay low. See you tomorrow.'

'Hang on,' Jordan almost begged. But Anand had rung off, giving Jordan no chance to share his bad news. Now he felt angry with Anand as well, for getting into this hole in the first place and for dragging Jordan down with him. He felt sure they hadn't seen the end of the business with the footie crew. What an idiot his friend had been. He realised right now there was no point looking to

Anand for any sympathy, given his own problems.

Jordan found himself savagely itching his eczema and, even when he realised, he didn't stop, because he didn't care. Let it get infected; let him end up in hospital; things couldn't be any worse. He was distracted for a moment by the sound of rain lashing on the windows. It was pouring down and he'd left his trainers outside the back door. Well, that was tough, too! It wasn't his fault he'd virtually been mugged.

He was just weighing up whether to ring Martine – he'd probably have to hear all about the wedding first, but maybe afterwards she at least might give him a bit of sympathy back – when he heard his dad tap on the door.

'Are you awake?' he whispered.

Jordan didn't reply but his dad came in anyway. He was holding the phone again. 'Please have a word with your mum. She's ever so worried about you.'

Jordan ground his teeth together. It was a bad habit he'd got into lately; even Martine had remarked on it.

He held his hand out for the phone. 'I'm in bed, Mum,' he said, trying to sound sleepy but just sounding grumpy.

'I'm sorry, love, I didn't mean to disturb you,' she apologised. 'I just haven't talked to you much in days. I really miss you, Jordie.'

Jordan felt horrible. He knew she meant it, which made it so much harder to understand. 'Look, I'll come up tomorrow,' he promised, desperate to get her off the phone.

That was all she needed to hear. 'Goodnight, sweetheart. I love you,' she said and rang off. Jordan handed the phone back to his dad, who'd been standing over his bed, watching him keenly.

'Are you all right?' he asked, sitting down on the edge of the bed.

Jordan sighed. Of course he wasn't all right. 'I want her home,' he said, and caught his breath before a sob followed hot on his words.

'I know, lad,' his dad replied, moving forward to hug him, but Jordan realised this would undo him. He sat back out of reach. He let his dad think he was too big for that sort of thing.

'You know it wasn't an easy decision for her?' his dad said.

'Did you and Kyle persuade her?' Jordan asked.

'No, of course not! It was her choice, but she didn't make it lightly. She can't wait to be home with you.'

'*So why's she doing it?*' Jordan almost sobbed.

'Well, after what she's been through, you can't blame her for wanting a bit more for herself, especially now she's not going to get into the record book. I think she feels it's her reward. And, you know, it really isn't very much longer.'

'Stop saying that!' Jordan yelled. 'It's ten more days!'

'I know.' His dad gave his arm a squeeze. 'Don't you think I won't be thanking God when it's all over?'

Jordan could see how much his dad meant that, how tired he looked, how weary with it all. 'So, why didn't you tell her that?' he asked. 'She'd come out if you asked her to.'

'That wouldn't be fair, would it? It's got to be her choice. The way I see it: we all have to help her finish the job she's started. And I mean a*ll of us*.'

Jordan knew that was directed at him. 'I just wish I could understand *why* she's doing it at all.'

'You know very well why,' his dad laughed. 'She wanted to do something to make herself feel special – her moment of fame, I suppose. So people would notice her.'

Jordan groaned. It was all people talked about these days – *being famous*. But other people who wanted to be famous did things like go on *Big Brother*. They didn't do something as weird as his mum – nobody else would have chosen to be *buried for five months*.

'Anyway, you need to get some sleep,' his dad told

him. 'You've got school tomorrow. And so have I. I've got to see your form teacher. I hope to God you've been trying a bit harder. I don't want to have to tell your mum things have got any worse.'

His dad studied him, as if looking for some hint of what to expect, but Jordan couldn't return his dad's gaze. He felt guilty. His dad had enough on his plate without all Jordan's troubles at school.

Bending down to give him a kiss, his dad said, 'You still smell of fish. Have you had a wash?'

'*Yes*,' Jordan said, too sharply.

His dad wasn't fooled. 'By the way, you left your trainers outside in all that rain. I only found them when I let the dog out. They were soaked through and smelled disgusting, as if you'd been paddling in the river. I've packed them with newspaper and put them on the boiler. You won't be wearing those tomorrow.'

Jordan nodded and kept his head down. That was a narrow escape.

Before he turned out the light he checked the time. It was probably too late to ring Martine, but he could text and find out.

'*R U still awake?*'

The reply came swiftly: a text with a smilie face.

Jordan rang and Martine answered immediately.

She sounded as if she was in bed, too, and almost asleep.

'So, how was the wedding?'

'Gross. What d'you expect? Got my revenge, though: I got Coke down one dress and ripped the other doing the splits!!!'

Jordan almost forgot his pledge with Anand and admitted they'd seen that.

'At least it's all over for you,' he said instead.

'Sure is. They've all gone off on honeymoon and left me in peace. I'm at my dad's till after Christmas now. It's going to be fan-tastic!'

Jordan went absolutely silent at this reminder of his own troubles.

'You still there?' Martine asked.

'Mmm,' he muttered.

'Well, there's only a couple of days left for you now, buddy.'

Suddenly Jordan couldn't even find the energy to enlighten his friend. He decided to save that piece of bad news for tomorrow.

'Going,' he told her. 'Catch you at school.'

He lay in bed trying to find some small scrap of hope to hang onto. He tried to persuade himself that, contrary to what his dad had told him, this new plan

205

was not really his mum's choice. She *must* have been persuaded into it, if not by his dad and his brother, then by that slimy reporter. The more Jordan thought about it the more likely it seemed. He couldn't bring himself to believe that after so long she would willingly choose to stay down there rather than be back home – with him. Maybe, with a bit of encouragement, she might still change her mind.

It was a small glimmer of hope but just enough to calm him until he finally managed to drift into sleep.

CHAPTER SIXTEEN

He was digging again, still trying to find his way out. He'd changed direction so many times he had a feeling he was going round in circles. Each time he felt close to penetrating the surface – just as he could almost smell the air above him – a new layer of soil was dumped on his head.

With each new frustration he dug more and more slowly and with less determination. He was close to giving up, when a giant hand reached down and plucked him out of the ground.

Jordan was suddenly awake and automatically reaching for his phone before he realised it hadn't been that that had woken him. It wasn't even ringing. He turned over and pulled the quilt over his head. He couldn't be bothered to get up. What was the point?

But then he remembered that little glimmer of hope again. It was enough to get him up and out of the house. He was already taking Jet round the block when his wake-up call came.

'Good morning, sweetie,' his mum said. 'Time to get up.'

'Already up,' he told her. 'I'm coming to see you in a minute. Do you need anything?'

'Nothing else,' she said, 'just my favourite boy.' Jordan could tell by her voice how much she meant it. It took so little on his part to please her that he wished he'd been able to do it more often.

He rode up the hill to the farm with a new sense of energy. He left his bike outside the barrier, which was still down, and called to let her know he was there. 'Morning, Mum.' He could hear his voice sounding much more like his old self.

'Hello, my darling,' she said, sounding quite cheerful as well.

Jordan was careful not to come right out with his idea. 'So how are you doing?'

'Yeah, good,' she said. 'Getting a bit stiffer by the day. My circulation doesn't seem to be working; I keep getting these numb hands; I probably need to do more exercises. They're so boring, though, the same thing every day. Anyway, what do you think about the holiday ideas?'

Jordan shrugged. 'Yeah, OK, I s'pose.'

'Don't get too excited,' she teased him.

'It's just…you don't have to do it for us, you know. I'm not that bothered about holidays.'

'I know I don't,' she laughed. 'The money'll be great, but that's just the icing on the cake. It's the fact they're going to make such a big splash in the papers, with it being New Year and everything. We'll get loads more coverage.'

'But if your circulation's bad…' Jordan persisted.

'Oh, don't worry about me, sweetie. I'll be glad to be out, of course, but it's not so bad.'

'I don't know how you can say that,' he told her sharply.

'I suppose I've got used to it now. Once everyone goes away and leaves me in peace, I quite like having the time to myself. *You* must understand that.'

Jordan blinked. 'What do you mean?' Why would *he* understand?

'Well, it's like when you're off fishing, just being inside your own head. It's quite peaceful at times.'

Jordan couldn't begin to see the comparison. He was really starting to think his mum was plain selfish. Didn't she have any idea how much everyone else was having to give up? His dad never had a minute to himself; Kyle was devoting hours every week to supporting her; his aunt waited on her hand and foot. Plus she had to be pleasant to all the weird people who came up here to witness the freak show. And what about him? What about all the emotional fallout in his family – its split down the middle – and all for what? For his mum to lie there chasing some pitiful record that in a few months' time *everyone* would have forgotten about. And then having the nerve to tell him that she quite liked having the time to herself!

She was always saying how much she was missing him, but where was the evidence? If it *was* true, she'd be coming out tomorrow as she'd first promised. It was suddenly too much for Jordan. If he hung around another minute longer he definitely would lose it and not be able to keep the promise he'd made everyone not to upset his mum.

'Gotta go,' he said, no longer sounding in the least bit cheerful.

'See you later, sweetie.'

As he swung onto his bike, he asked himself angrily: *What is the matter with you*? How could he have let himself build up his hopes *again*? He must be mad, he thought.

When he got into school, and found Anand yet again cosying up to Jason Carlisle and the others, Jordan finally did lose it. His friend was handing out sweets and ciggies, as if yesterday had never happened. The boys crowded round him, arguing about who was getting most. Jordan was ready to shake some sense into his friend's thick skull and he went over planning to do just that.

'What d'you think you're playing at?' he asked, straight out.

'Chill out,' Anand laughed, clearly embarrassed. 'Cool it, man.'

'No, you cool it,' Jordan yelled at him. 'What are you doing still stealing from your own dad to keep these morons happy?'

'Keep your voice down,' Anand begged him. 'It's nothing.'

'It's not *nothing*,' Jordan yelled again. 'It's wrong. It's not *fair*.'

Fair? Was that the best he could come up with? Jordan knew he was embarrassing himself, but somehow he couldn't stop. 'You can't let them get away with it,' he said through gritted teeth. 'You can't let them push you around.'

The boys looked at him with disgust, as if he were a baby about to burst out crying, which he felt shamefully close to doing.

Anand looked at him under his eyebrows. 'For God's sake, stop it,' he hissed at Jordan. 'Get over yourself.'

'OK, go with them,' Jordan warned, 'but don't come running to me next time they threaten to beat you up. Don't drag me into your pathetic fights *ever again.*'

'Oh, get lost! You're boring, man,' Anand told him. 'All you do these days is whinge. Who needs it?' And he walked off with the other boys, leaving Jordan feeling even lower than before, if that were possible.

Martine was sitting on her desk happily eating a packet of M&Ms. Jordan gave her a dirty look too. She rolled her eyes. 'Don't worry, you don't have to say anything, it's all over. I've given up bingeing. Just one packet a day now, or maybe two,' she grinned. Jordan looked sceptical. 'I was just trying to make a point, dumbo,' she told him. 'I wasn't going to let them rule my life. Anyway, now the stupid weddings are over I don't need to.'

Jordan shrugged. He didn't know if he could believe her, but he was past worrying about anyone else.

'You know you're wasting your time,' Martine said, nodding in Anand's direction. 'I've told you before, it's like an addiction. He's not gonna change until he decides he wants to.'

Jordan shrugged again and dumped his bag on the floor. He joined Martine on the desk and, taking the packet out of her hands, emptied a load of sweets into his own. 'She's not coming out,' he told her.

'Not *ever*?' Martine asked.

'Of course, *ever*, just not before Christmas. She's added another ten days, until New Year.'

'What a drag,' Martine sympathised. 'Perhaps she's getting too used to it, you know, like people who never go out of the house. Maybe she's agoraphobic.'

'Cheer me up, why don't you?' Jordan said.

'Well, think about it – she'd need a pretty good reason to want to stay there any longer than she had to.'

'Ten thousand pounds?' Jordan suggested.

Martine's eyes blinked like they were flashing pound signs. 'That's a pretty good reason.'

Jordan had conveniently forgotten that it was this evening his dad was coming in to see Mrs Raynsworth and that she had expressly told him to bring a selection of his coursework to her at lunchtime. So when she was forced to send someone onto the playground to find him, she was already coming up to the boil. When he arrived empty-handed she blew her lid.

'You really are the limit, Jordan. Don't imagine I'll be pulling my punches this evening. I shall tell your father that, despite all the warnings since October, your work – and your general behaviour – has gone steadily downhill. I just hope when it's all over you can manage to turn it around, I really do.'

Jordan was barely even listening. It wasn't that he was deliberately stopping himself from feeling things – his teacher's disappointment, the quite reasonable anxiety he might feel about his dad's reaction – but nothing was actually touching him.

He spent the whole afternoon in cookery working on his own. When Martine walked into the room and saw Anand already unpacking his bag in one corner and Jordan in another, she hesitated. She clearly didn't like having to choose between her friends, but as she told Jordan, 'I'm sorry, but cookery's always a laugh and he's right, you do whinge a bit at the moment.'

Jordan didn't argue with her. He was sick of his own company and would have walked away himself given half a chance. They were making Chelsea buns and Jordan kept his head down, taking out some of his frustration on the dough. As he stretched and folded it, then punched it back into a ball, he kept telling himself that he had to *do* something. There had to be one small part of his miserable life that he could still actually fix.

While he waited for the oven to come to temperature, he looked across the room and saw Nutter Norris and Jason Carlisle pushing Anand about again. They made it look like it was all some big joke; he could see Anand smiling, but Jordan recognised that smile and he hated it.

He looked like one of those animals in wildlife programmes – the weak ones in the pack – that lie down on the ground and show their belly as a sign of submission. Anand wasn't exactly lying on the home economics room floor exposing his stomach, but he was giving off the same signals.

That was the final straw for Jordan. If Anand wouldn't stand up to these bullies and stop thieving, Jordan would have to make him. He couldn't stand by and watch his friend get in any deeper. He had to do *something*.

After school Jordan walked Jet round the streets, ending up on Anand's road. He hung around for a while, letting Jet sniff a few lampposts, until he saw the person he was waiting for: Vaishali, Anand's older sister, walking down the road with a couple of her sixth-form college friends. When he started to follow her, Vaishali turned and gave him a warning look.

'I just want to talk to you,' he said.

All the other girls started to laugh at him, but Vaishali wasn't amused. 'What do you want?' she demanded.

Jordan felt entirely intimidated by the older girls and the way they were staring at him. He blushed and finally managed to ask, 'Can I talk to you for a minute...on your own?'

Jordan hadn't worked out exactly what he was going to say. All he knew was that he needed someone close to Anand – not his mum or dad, of course, but someone older to talk some sense into him. He knew that Anand considered Vaishali the least annoying of his brothers and sisters. She seemed really cool and

Jordan felt sure she'd be able to make him see sense, before things got any worse.

But when Jordan had told her the story Vaishali looked so angry he began to feel as if she held him responsible.

'Why have you done nothing before now?' she demanded. 'Why haven't you stopped him? You're supposed to be his friend.'

Jordan hung his head. When it first started he probably had been too wrapped up in his own troubles to help, and now it felt too late. 'He won't listen to me,' he told her. 'He might listen to you, though.'

'He'd better, the lamebrain,' she almost spat out. 'Wait till our dad finds out.'

Jordan's mouth flew open in horror. 'You won't tell him?' he begged.

'Are you kidding? He's the only person that can make my brainless brother see sense.'

'But I'd never have told you if I thought...' Jordan started.

But Vaishali cut him off. 'Well, maybe if you'd done the right thing earlier it wouldn't have come to this.' And she walked away, leaving him stunned.

Jordan would have cut his tongue out before dumping his friend in it with his dad. Anand would never forgive him now. Jordan had managed to make a bad situation so much worse. He yanked Jet's lead and dragged the poor dog away, making him feel as if he had done something wrong.

As he went into the house his dad was just leaving, wearing a jacket and an unaccustomed tie that he was still struggling to fasten. Jordan could see his dad had cut himself shaving.

'There's pizza in the oven,' he told Jordan. 'Kyle's making some chips. I'm late for Mrs Raynsworth, which won't create a good impression.'

His dad looked more nervous than Jordan at the prospect of facing his form tutor. He felt really guilty that his dad was going to hear a long list of bad things about Jordan that would upset him, things he would probably have to keep from his mum. It felt as if everything Jordan touched at the moment turned bad.

Over tea, even though the chips weren't cooked properly, Jordan said nothing to provoke an argument with Kyle. Soon his brother was on his way out, too.

'Any messages for Mum?' he asked as he left.

'Say hi,' Jordan replied.

'Is that it?' Kyle asked scornfully.

'I was up there this morning,' Jordan told him.

The truth was a lot of things had happened since

then, but nothing he wanted to share with his mum.

Jordan mooched around the house all evening, not able to settle. He sat at the table with his homework book open, as if this might soften the blow when his dad came in and saw him apparently turning over a new leaf. But it was just for show. By the time his dad came home, Jordan still hadn't written a word.

He didn't know whether to expect fireworks or a big lecture or both. But his dad just came and sat at the table with him, looking completely defeated.

'Oh, Jordan, I don't even know what to say to you. Could you not have just hung in there until the end of term? I really don't need to have you to worry about at the moment.'

Jordan hung his head. He didn't bother offering any excuses.

'I'm not going to tell your mum any of it; I don't want to worry her. But you have to promise me that for the last two days of term you won't do anything stupid.'

Jordan looked at his dad and wondered what kind of stupid thing he had in mind.

'Your teacher seems to think you're very unhappy,' his dad said, looking genuinely concerned. 'Are you?'

Jordan almost snorted. Of course he was unhappy!

Any fool could see that. But what was the point of even talking about it? Like his dad said, it was just a waiting game now.

He didn't answer the question, so his dad asked him again, 'Promise me you'll just keep your head down and not cause any more trouble. Do *nothing* to rock the boat, OK?'

Jordan nodded. He wished his dad had asked for that promise a couple of hours ago, before he threw a hand grenade into his friend's life.

'Now, it's only for ten more days,' his dad finished off. 'I want you to get straight on the phone and let your mum know that you're all right and completely on board with the plan.'

Jordan nodded. He had no option. He went up to his bedroom and looked for his phone. When he saw the pile of Christmas presents he'd already wrapped he kicked them around his room and then threw them angrily in the back of his wardrobe. He just wanted to sleep through Christmas and wake up for the New Year. It had to be better than this one, surely.

Jordan lay on his bed and rang his mum's number. He swallowed back the tears as he heard her voice. 'Oh, it's my gorgeous boy. How are you, sweetheart? Have you had a good day? Tell me all about it.'

CHAPTER SEVENTEEN

It took a lot of courage for Jordan to go round to collect Anand next morning, having no idea what kind of reception he would get. But he at least needed to try to explain to his friend why he'd done it.

Jordan walked into the shop and looked around, hoping to see Anand before Anand's dad spotted him, but neither was in the shop. Anand's mum was behind the till, and when she looked at Jordan he couldn't tell what, if anything, she knew. But Anand's mum was very shy and only ever gave Jordan a quick smile, so there was no clue there.

'Is Anand ready?' he asked. She shook her head, offering no explanation, even though he waited for one.

As soon as Jordan arrived in school he searched for Martine to ask if she'd seen Anand yet. 'Nope. Didn't you call for him?'

Jordan nodded. 'He wasn't there.'

'So where is he?'

It was registration time; he was certainly going to be late. Jordan sighed and told Martine exactly what he had done the day before and what he now feared Anand's sister had done with the information he'd given her.

'Oh, you blockhead! You are one mental case,' she told him. 'What were you thinking of?'

'I know, I know.' Jordan put up his hands, conceding defeat. 'I just thought someone had to stop him.'

'*Yeah*, but that someone didn't need to be his dad! You know what he's like. He could teach Attilla the Hun a few tricks. I bet Anand's locked in his bedroom on bread and water *as we speak*.'

Jordan put his hands over his ears. He couldn't bear to hear any more. He knew he'd made a big mistake; he didn't need Martine rubbing it in.

'Where's Skanki?' Jason Carlisle asked at break time, but Jordan shrugged. He wouldn't have given his friend's torturers any information, even if he had it.

Jordan didn't know how he was going to get through the day not knowing Anand's fate. Just being in school seemed so pointless. Why didn't they realise you couldn't expect kids to concentrate and do any real work in the last couple of days of term, especially in the run-up to Christmas? Why couldn't they pack up shop and let everyone – teachers and kids alike – clear off home and save themselves the bother?

The morning dragged until lunchtime, when he was free to text Anand and try to track him down. But when three texts sent in quick succession brought no response, Jordan made his way to his afternoon lessons in a very low mood. He sat through maths letting the teacher's explanation of quadratic equations drift over his head while he daydreamed – about fishing, of course.

He was on the riverbank, with his grandpa, just after his eighth birthday, when he'd got his own first fishing rod. His grandpa had baited it up for him and settled Jordan before setting up his own line. Suddenly Jordan had squealed, 'Grandpa, quick, I've got something!' His grandpa had yelled, 'Hold tight!' but Jordan had been so surprised he'd lost his grip on the rod, and it and the line had fallen into the water and gone sailing down the river – his new first fishing rod.

It had taken his grandpa more than an hour to retrieve the rod and almost as long to disentangle it. They had had to walk half a mile to reach the opposite bank, and then do a lot of casting and gentle manoeuvring to pull it in. Jordan had thought that would be the last time his grandpa ever took him fishing; he'd certainly moaned enough while it was going on. But when they got home he'd made such a brilliant story of it and retold it for weeks – to Jordan's embarrassment.

When his grandpa had finally handed him the rod back, he'd told Jordan, 'Never let go of your line, OK? Next time hang onto it, even if it means falling in yourself.' It seemed strange advice from someone who claimed to have never fallen in the water over a whole lifetime of fishing.

Jordan was looking out of the window, wishing with all his heart he was down by the river now. He hated this time of year, when the days were so short that there was no chance to fish after school. While his grandpa was alive they'd occasionally fished in the dark; night fishing was a real buzz. But his mum and dad absolutely refused to let Jordan go fishing – on his own – in the dark.

When he was older he would go off for weekends

with a little tent and lie in his sleeping bag with his rod sticking out the end and fish all through the night, as his grandpa sometimes did, letting his bait alarm wake him if he got a bite. It sounded like heaven to Jordan.

For almost half an hour – most of the lesson, in fact – Jordan had lost all sense of where he was. He suddenly came to when the people around him drew back their chairs. He picked up his bag and walked out, following the drift of other kids towards the next lesson. He was stopped in his tracks when he saw Martine waiting for him in the corridor with a murderous look on her face.

'His dad's here!' she announced dramatically.

Jordan had been so far away, almost on another planet, that he wondered for a moment whose father she could be talking about. His mystified face really infuriated her.

'Anand's dad, *dummy*. I've just seen him going into the office. He looked mad as a bag of skunks. *You* are for it.'

Jordan was fully awake now and already processing the full implications of this piece of news. 'Anand's never going to forgive me for this,' he moaned.

'Never,' Martine agreed.

'Oh, God,' he groaned.

'Too late for divine intervention,' she said, not even trying to soften the blow. 'Where are you going now?' she asked, as Jordan started down the corridor. He'd been heading for the office to see for himself, but Martine yanked him back. 'What's the point? Nothing you can do now – except hope,' she advised.

'I've been trying to text him...' Jordan told her. 'But he's not answering.'

'I know, me too,' Martine replied. 'Bad sign.'

It certainly was. Anand was usually inseparable from his phone.

Jordan and Martine went into the next lesson, which was English, and sat down together. Ten minutes later the door opened and the secretary entered, asking for Carlisle, Norris and Ransom to go directly to the head's office. Jordan watched the boys leave the room. They looked completely surprised. They weren't so stupid that they couldn't work out it probably meant trouble, but out of sheer bravado they behaved as if they'd won the lottery and the head had been given the privilege of presenting them with the cheque.

Jordan turned to Martine, who simply drew her finger across her throat and made an unpleasant cutting sound.

'Do you prefer black or white grapes?' she asked. When Jordan looked confused she added, 'When I visit you in hospital.'

By the end of the lesson, when the boys hadn't returned, Martine gave Jordan some more helpful advice. 'I'd get off now, if I were you, before they get out. Oh, and I'd stay in bed tomorrow. It's *possible* that by next term they'll have forgotten all about it. But then again – not likely.'

Jordan looked so paralysed for a moment that Martine suddenly felt sorry for him. 'Look, d'you want me to come home with you?' she asked. 'Only I thought I'd call in at the shop, see if I can find out anything.'

Jordan shook his head. 'It's fine.' He'd be quicker on his own. 'But let me know if there's any news.'

He raced out of school, almost knocking people over in his rush to get to the bike shed. But as he turned the corner he slowed right down. The boys were already waiting for him, and he was in no hurry to confront them.

'You and that skanky little friend of yours are dead meat,' Jason told him.

'It's not Anand's fault,' Jordan admitted. 'It was me that shopped you.'

'Oh, we already worked that out. Don't worry, we'll make sure you get the biggest kicking.'

Other kids were coming to collect their bikes, and Jordan somehow knew they weren't going to do it in front of an audience. They'd choose their moment, probably reporting back to Connor Stewart and Ricky Doherty first. He felt as if he'd brought the whole thing upon himself, and that in a way he deserved a good kicking, but it didn't stop him from feeling terrified. He suddenly had more sympathy with Anand and his lurid fantasies about what the boys might do; Jordan was having a couple of his own right now. But he wasn't expecting what Jason Carlisle said next.

'How's your mum doing, Gibbo? She must get pretty lonely up there – in the middle of the night.'

Nutter Norris grinned. 'You never did tell us what was the weirdest thing anyone ever dropped down the pipe,' he reminded him.

The caretaker, old Bennett, came walking across the yard. He could always spot an unhealthy grouping of troublemakers.

'Anyway, we'll be seeing *you* – very soon,' Jason promised.

'Or someone close to you,' Nutter Norris grinned.

'You got no homes to go to?' the caretaker asked pointedly.

The boys didn't even look at him, but they started to move off.

'Gotta go. Gotta take a leak,' they told Jordan.

'Lay an egg...'

'Drop a bomb...'

'Block a drain...'

'Flush one down...'

The boys kept up their list of toilet euphemisms all the way across the playground, until they were out of earshot. Mr Bennett looked Jordan up and down and gave him an enquiring look, but Jordan kept his mouth firmly closed. He'd learned that lesson. He rode home the long way, where he wouldn't be likely to meet any of his tormentors again.

Jordan knew that he should go straight home and see to the dog, but all he could think about was his mum. He had to go up there and warn her, but if those morons were only bluffing the last thing he wanted to do was put ideas into her head. It might remind her about that other time, and make her decide to come out. Obviously, nothing would have suited him better, but he didn't want to get his mum home that way – by frightening her almost to death. He tried to convince himself the boys had just been trying to scare him. Well, if that had been their aim they'd certainly managed it.

Jordan got off his bike and saw a short line of people queuing to visit his mum. He wasn't going to wait his turn, so he put his head round the door of the café and gave his aunt a look. She came straight out and dispersed the queue, offering people a free cup of tea while they waited.

'This is a nice surprise,' his mum told him. 'How was school?'

School was the last thing Jordan wanted to talk about, especially the last half-hour of it. He tried to steer the conversation in a different direction.

'Mum, what's it like, when you're down there at night and everybody's gone home. D'you ever get lonely?'

'Not lonely exactly.'

'Don't you miss Dad?'

'Course I do,' she laughed, 'even his cold feet. I don't miss his snoring, though.'

Jordan groaned. Parents could be so embarrassing.

'I suppose that's the time when it feels most real,' she said. 'In the daytime I can hear other people and sort of feel them up there. It's only at night I get to think about the fact that there's several tonnes of soil above me and imagine what it would be like...' She trailed off, as if she didn't want to admit to Jordan what went through her mind in her darkest moments.

But Jordan wanted to know. 'Do you get scared?' he asked. It was a risky question. He really didn't want to be worrying her, but he needed to know.

She thought about it for a moment. 'Of course,' she said, much more lightly. 'There've been plenty of times I've felt scared, but they've passed. Anyway, being scared's no good reason for not doing something. And I'm past the worst part now; I just have to see it through.'

'You don't *have* to,' Jordan argued.

'I do, sweetheart, because I'm someone who sticks at things. If I say I'm gong to do something... I'm determined – like your grandpa.'

'*Stubborn, you mean,*' his gran would have said if she'd been there. She claimed it ran in the family. 'Your grandpa was like a blimmin' old donkey,' she used to say. 'Nobody could budge him once he'd made up his mind.'

Jordan wanted to go on arguing the point with his mum, but he knew it was no use; she was the same – immovable.

'Is it raining?' she suddenly asked.

Jordan looked out from the shelter. 'I think it's snowing.'

'It was forecast for today. Maybe we're going to have a white Christmas.'

'No chance,' Jordan said grumpily. 'They always talk about white Christmases, but I've never seen one.' Part of him believed they were like fairy stories made up by adults to entertain children, like the Tooth Fairy or the Easter Bunny. Anyway, what difference did it make whether there was a white Christmas, he thought, if his mum was still down there?

'You should get off home before it really sets in,' she told him.

But Jordan didn't want to go. How could he leave her, not knowing she'd be safe? How could he warn her to be careful, without telling her why? He considered talking to his aunt. He could say he'd heard some boys joking about coming up here at night. But he knew it would turn into the Spanish Inquisition, thumbscrews and all, until she had their names and addresses out of him. He'd already made the mistake over Anand of opening his mouth and turning a small matter between kids into a bigger one that involved adults. His common sense told him not to do that again.

In the end Jordan went off home, knowing at least that for the next few hours there'd be visitors with his mum, then his dad would arrive. She'd be OK – for now, anyway.

Before he got on his bike he checked his phone and found three messages from Martine already, telling him there was no news about Anand but wanting to know if he'd got home in one piece – or five hundred! He texted back, telling her, no sweat – they were all talk.

Jordan wished he felt half as confident as his text sounded.

After supper Jordan's dad sat and watched ten minutes of the news before his eyes began to close. Jordan sat watching him, debating the possibility of telling his dad how worried he was. But how could he explain the boys' threats without giving the whole background story, and breaking his promise to Anand again.

He couldn't honestly believe they'd been serious. He told himself he was probably worrying about nothing. If only he could be sure.

'Da-a-ad.' Jordan shook him. 'Isn't it time you were going up to see Mum?'

'Oh, yeah,' his dad yawned. He clearly wasn't in

a hurry to go out into the freezing cold night. The snow wasn't sticking yet, but it was still falling steadily.

'Can I come with you?'

'I shouldn't, lad, not tonight. It's bitter cold out there. I shan't be staying long myself.'

'I think you should, Dad,' Jordan told him.

'You've changed your tune. Who's the slave driver now, then?'

'I just think she must get lonely at night.'

'Yeah, well, I've been telling you that these past few weeks when you've been so reluctant to go up there.'

'I know,' Jordan admitted, guiltily.

'Well, once you've broken up tomorrow you can spend more time with her, eh? Help her get through the last stretch.'

Jordan nodded. *Stretch* was the right word for it. It made it sound like a prison sentence, which was exactly what it had felt like for him, and he didn't think he'd done anything to deserve it – until now. But this would be his punishment: as soon as school broke up he'd have to act as permanent bodyguard to his mum, because it was perfectly possible that those imbeciles would be looking for some form of amusement – and he was determined *she* wasn't going to provide it.

CHAPTER EIGHTEEN

For the next hour Jordan watched TV, wrapping himself around Jet for warmth and a bit of comfort. He'd tried once again to text Anand and this time a reply came immediately, but it hadn't cheered him up in the least. It was a long message, and although it came from Anand's phone it was sent by his dad: '*I am afraid my son may not correspond with you. He is in much disgrace. He is the black dog of the family and has had a severe grounding.*'

Jordan dropped his phone as if it were red hot. When he'd got over the shock of it, he thought about ringing Martine. But he had no good news about Anand, and he was afraid that if he actually spoke to her he'd tell her what the boys had hinted at about his mum. If he did that he knew it would feel more real, and he would end up in an even bigger panic. He was just about managing to keep a lid on it by convincing himself it *was* all talk.

Instead he channel-hopped, trying to find something that would distract him. It seemed no time at all before he heard his dad letting himself back in. Kyle was with him.

'You didn't stay long,' Jordan said accusingly. 'Who's with Mum?'

'She's fine. She said she wanted to have an early night,' his dad replied.

'Anyway, it was too cold,' Kyle said. 'My feet were nearly dropping off.'

'You could wear those boots of Grandpa's,' Jordan suggested. His grandpa had a fishing pair with battery-operated heating systems inside.

'Thanks,' Kyle said, 'but I'll pass for tonight. I'm off for a bath.'

His dad turned over the channel to watch a boxing match, so Jordan went up to bed. He rang his mum, and even though she sounded sleepy, kept her chatting on the other end of the phone as long as he could.

'Are you all right, Jordan?' she asked him at one point.

'Yeah, why?'

'You sound a bit…hyper.' His mum yawned. 'Better get to bed, duck, you've got one more day at school yet.'

'Half a day,' he corrected her.

'Yeah, well, you still need to be up in the morning. Goodnight, my darling.'

'Hang on, Mum, don't go.'

'What is it?'

'Nothing. Just wanted to say…I love you.'

'I love you too. Goodnight.'

As soon as she rang off, Jordan wanted to call her straight back and keep her on the phone – for the whole night if he had to. He tried to reassure himself that his mum wasn't totally alone: his uncle and aunt were only one hundred metres away, with an alarm connected to their bedroom; they could be with her in minutes, even in the middle of the night.

But when he thought how little time it would take for someone to do something really horrible, or even just terrify her, he didn't feel a bit reassured. He couldn't bear to think of his mum being scared – and on her own – all because of him.

Jordan drifted into sleep but had one of his falling dreams, where he dropped like a bucket down a well.

When he woke he was clutching onto his quilt to save himself. He almost cried out for his dad, but just stopped himself. He lay in a terrible sweat, feeling sick. When he reached for his phone and checked the time it was 1.30. The house was completely silent.

Jordan's heart was racing and he thought this must be what a panic attack was like. This must be what his mum had felt in the very first days she was buried – and yet she still hadn't given up. How brave she'd been.

He lay there, unable to shake off the terrible feeling that something was wrong. Suddenly, he sat up in bed, knowing what he had to do. He had to go up there – now – and check she was OK. If he rang it would frighten her and he'd still need to explain everything. This was a better plan: he wouldn't need to wake her, but simply reassure himself that nothing was wrong, then come home. No one would even have to know.

Jordan got out of bed and started to get dressed. He knew he was probably being completely stupid, but he needed to see for himself that, even though she was buried, his mum was still alive.

When he reached the farm, Jordan left his bike halfway down the hill; he couldn't risk waking his aunt and uncle. He knew getting across the gravel was going to be a nightmare; it surely had to be the best burglar alarm in the world. He hadn't brought a torch, but there were a couple of security lights around the nursery, so he could just see where he was going. He took a few hesitant steps, then bit by bit he slowly made his way across the car park.

When he finally reached the shelter he relaxed and let out the breath he'd been holding until now. He carefully climbed over the turnstile then crouched down, leaning his back against the wall of the shelter, waiting for his heart to stop racing and wondering what to do next.

Now that he was here he realised what a crazy idea it had been. What had he expected to find? Had he really believed those idiots would have come up here in the middle of the night – especially a night as cold as this? He had to face facts: he didn't have any kind of plan. He was definitely losing it. Jordan began berating himself in just the way his dad would if he caught him now: '*What were you thinking of, lad? What are you doing here? What's the matter with you? Are you mad?*'

Jordan knew that he couldn't possibly stay for long – it was far too cold. But he stubbornly crouched there, hugging himself, and thought about his mum lying directly beneath him, just six feet of soil between them. All the times he'd visited he'd refused to let himself think that one day she would be down there – for good – in a real grave. His head started shaking from side to side, as if it were saying, don't even think about that; she's not dead!

He leaned over and put his head above the pipe and listened hard. He tried to still his own breath so that he could hear *her* breathing. He waited what seemed like minutes before he heard a sound echoing inside the pipe, somewhere between a breath and a snore. It was coming regularly now, like a heartbeat, and seemed to match the pulse beating behind his own ear. He leaned closer and reached down into the pipe. He knew it was fruitless – his arm would never reach that far; but Jordan had a desperate desire to try to touch his mum.

He suddenly straightened up. Just the thought of it had caused a sensation in his chest, like a lump rising, and he thought he might be sick. But he realised it wasn't vomit; it was a sob. No, more than a sob – a wail deep inside determined to get out. He put his hand over his mouth to keep it in, but the need to wail was taking over his whole body and he couldn't hold it back.

He was really shivering now, and to steady himself Jordan gripped the iron turnstile, causing the metal frame to creak noisily. He quickly let it go, as if it had burned him, setting the noise off again.

He leaned back and crouched lower, as if trying to hide himself, and stayed as still and silent as a stone. He listened hard, but there was nothing, no breathing now, and then he realised his mum was awake. What he could hear was the sound of someone holding their breath.

When her voice came, she sounded scared, but like someone trying to be brave: 'Who's there? I know someone's there. I can hear you. I've got a phone; I'm ringing the police; I'm ringing them now…'

Jordan knew the game was up. He couldn't bear to hear her sounding so scared. He also couldn't let her call the police. He leaned over the pipe and whispered, 'It's me, Mum; it's Jordan. I didn't mean to scare you.'

'*Jordan?*' she sounded incredulous. 'What on earth are you doing here? What time is it? What's happened?'

Jordan groaned, because now he could see lights coming on in the bungalow. What an unholy mess he'd caused. His uncle opened the front door and came out running, wearing his dressing gown and Wellingtons and carrying a big torch, which he was swinging like a truncheon. Jordan just wanted the ground to open up and bury him – alongside his mum.

His uncle screwed up his eyes, trying to make out who was there. He clearly couldn't believe what he was seeing.

'*Jordan*, what on earth are you doing here? It's two o'clock in the morning. What's happened? Is your mum OK?'

She called out before Jordan had time to speak. 'I'm OK, Matt. I didn't realise it was Jordan. I'm really sorry we've woken you.'

His uncle was still waiting for some kind of explanation, but Jordan faced him out, refusing to give way.

'What are you doing here?' his uncle asked again, really angry now.

Jordan almost spat out the reply. 'I'm talking to my mother, for God's sake! If that's anything to do with you?'

'Jordan!' his mum gasped. She couldn't make any sense of what was happening from where she was, but his uncle could see the state Jordan was in. He didn't argue any more; he just turned and walked back to the house.

For a moment or two Jordan needed to calm himself

and push those sobs back down to where they'd been sitting for the last few weeks, but his mum was already pressing him: 'What's happening? Tell me, Jordan.'

'It's OK,' Jordan told her. 'He's gone back to bed. Oh, no he hasn't, he's coming back.' He braced himself for another difficult scene with his uncle, but he only handed Jordan a blanket to wrap round himself. Jordan realised then how very cold he'd got. He stamped his feet a few times until the feeling came back into them.

'Jordan, talk to me,' his mum begged again. 'Tell me what's going on, *please*.' He could hear she was close to tears, too.

'I needed to know you were OK,' he told her.

'Why wouldn't I be?'

Even now he couldn't bring himself to tell her about the football boys. 'I just wanted to talk to you.'

'*In the middle of the night?* About what?'

'I don't know,' he admitted, pathetically. He returned to his familiar question. 'Mum, why are you doing this?'

'Oh, Jordan,' she said wearily. 'How many more times? What else can I tell you, love? I wanted to be in the record books. It seemed important, at the time,' she said, sounding as if maybe it wasn't quite so important now. 'I know you can't understand that…'

'No,' he said sharply. He couldn't and he never would.

'But in any case, I can't give up now.'

'Why not?'

'I just can't. It'd be like giving in. I've got to show him…everybody,' she corrected herself.

'Show them what?'

His mum was quiet for a moment. 'That I'm as good as him, I suppose.'

Why was she talking in riddles?

'As good as who?' Jordan demanded.

'Your grandpa, of course. I suppose that's what it was always about: trying to be as good as him…but trying to be close to him as well.'

'Now you're *really* talking stupid,' Jordan snapped. 'How can you be close to him? He's not down there; he's on the bottom of the river. He didn't ever want to go back underground.'

'I know that, duck, but I thought by doing the same thing I'd *feel* closer to him, in a way I couldn't when he was alive.'

'And do you?' Jordan demanded.

'No, not really,' his mum admitted. She was quiet for a moment, then she suddenly started to wail in just the way he'd wanted to a few minutes earlier. 'Oh, Jordan, I can't bear it. I miss him, so much…'

His mum's tears didn't soften Jordan; he was feeling even more frustrated. 'You're not the only one who misses him, you know,' he told her. 'I miss him, but nothing like as much as I miss you.' Admitting this almost undid him. 'Grandpa's *dead*,' he said baldly, 'but you being in a grave isn't going to bring him back and…*it's not fair on the rest of us*!'

Suddenly those hidden sobs broke free, with all the added force of being denied for so long. 'I'm *sick* of waiting for you to come out. I don't *want* a holiday. I don't want a world record breaker for a mother. I want an ordinary mum and I want her home for Christmas!'

It was as if that simple truth suddenly released a whole string of complaints and misery that he'd been nursing for weeks. They came pouring out together: not only the things he wanted her to hear, but a lot more that he knew he'd regret in the morning. Everything: the stuff about school, the trouble with his form tutor, his poor grades, his worries about Martine and Anand. He told her about the football crew and how scared he'd been that they might have taken out their revenge on her. He admitted that was the real reason why he was here.

He told her how lonely he was at home, how much he missed her, his dad, his sister, his gran – his whole family. How much he hated his life and how there was no one who really understood. And when he'd finished Jordan realised it was just like being sick: horrible while it lasted, but a relief to get it all out of his system. And like being sick, it left him feeling cold and shaky. He wished more than anything that he was at home now in his own bed, with a hot-water bottle and his mum stroking his forehead until he went off to sleep.

His mum hadn't interrupted him once; she'd just listened in silence. At one point the lights had come on again in his aunt and uncle's bedroom and the window had opened, but then it was closed again and the house became completely dark.

Jordan knew he'd said too much, been too angry, mixed all the different bits up together, so probably none of it made any sense.

When his mum's voice came out of the darkness, it sounded as if she'd been crying too. 'Oh, Jordie, I had no idea. It breaks my heart to hear you like this. I'm so sorry. I wish I could put my arms round you.'

That was all Jordan wanted right now, too.

'Listen,' she went on, 'I'm going to ring your dad and get him to come and take you home...'

But Jordan begged her, 'No, Mum, please, please, don't ring Dad. He'll be so mad. Him and Kyle are gonna go crazy if they find out. They've been onto me for weeks about not upsetting you. Don't tell them. *Please!*'

'OK, but you must get off home now. You're going to catch your death otherwise and then you'll be the one in a wooden box,' she joked.

Jordan quickly got up. He folded the blanket and laid it over the top of the turnstile so it wouldn't get wet.

He hesitated for a moment, not sure what else to say. He was frantic that his mum shouldn't tell his dad. 'Mu-u-um...' he started.

'Just go straight home, darling. I shall be sick with worry till you're safely in bed. Ring me the minute you're back, OK?'

'OK,' he promised.

'I love you, darling,' she told him.

'I love you, Mum.'

'We'll talk tomorrow,' she said. 'And we'll sort it all out, I promise. Please don't worry any more.'

Jordan lay in bed unable to get warm. He'd got chilled to the bone and wet through on his way home. The snow had turned to rain, and it was pouring down again. He was wearing socks and a scarf and tracksuit bottoms over his pyjamas, but he still couldn't stop shaking. He had a horrible feeling this might have been an even bigger mistake than telling Anand's sister about his stealing from their dad.

He just wanted to go to sleep and stop thinking about it all. He wanted to forget he'd ever got out of bed and gone up there in the first place. He did drop off a couple of times, but then woke, feeling as if he were slipping off a ledge. Each time he immediately dropped back into sleep again, only to wake up within minutes. It was more than an hour before he'd fallen properly into an exhausted deep sleep and had another of the terrifying dreams he'd been having for so many months, but with a different twist altogether.

He wasn't buried underground, but everyone else was. All around him he could hear groans and cries for help. He was surrounded by heaps of rubble and collapsed buildings, as if there'd been an earthquake – or a bomb had gone off. From every direction he could hear voices calling him by name, although he couldn't recognise any of them. There were so many people trapped and only him left to get them out.

How could he possibly choose? Or even know where to start?

He looked around for something to dig with but there was nothing. So he started in the spot where he was standing, tearing off loose rubble with his hands, trying to reach the voice beneath him. But each time he got close to uncovering someone their cries disappeared, as if he'd arrived just moments too late. So he turned, following another still urgent cry somewhere nearby.

He'd been at it all day, and the thing he felt above all else was a desperate weariness. He just wanted to give up, and that was the thing that scared him most: the fact that if he stopped, no one would be saved. But the temptation to sleep was absolutely overpowering...

CHAPTER NINETEEN

Jordan was rescued from his dream by the sound of his brother yelling at him to get up. He looked at his phone and saw that it was only just after eight – not exactly late, but late for Kyle, who'd usually left for work by now.

'I won't tell you again,' Kyle shouted up the stairs. 'Get up – NOW!'

Jordan reluctantly threw back the duvet and found himself to be almost fully dressed. It took a moment for him to remember why. He felt as if he'd hardly slept at all. He was so tired he just wanted to hide under his bed until Kyle had gone, but his brother was charging up the stairs and throwing open his bedroom door.

'Get *up*,' he ordered, as if he were Jordan's dad or something, but a much more bad-tempered version.

'Who bit your bum?' Jordan asked, before he saw the thunderous expression on Kyle's face and knew not to provoke him any further.

'*You – bathroom!*' Kyle directed him.

Jordan sighed and dragged himself off. He locked the door and sat on the loo for as long as he thought he could get away with. Then he ran the taps for a few minutes to let Kyle think some washing had actually taken place. He went back to his bedroom, where his brother was still waiting for him.

'Shouldn't you be at work?' Jordan asked, in a neutral sort of voice.

'Yes – and so should Dad, but he isn't.'

Jordan looked up sharply. If his dad wasn't at work he had a good idea why; that explained why Kyle was ripping his ear off. 'He's not at work because he's had to go up and calm Mum down and sort out the mess *you* caused with your little night-time adventure.'

Jordan felt let down. He wasn't really surprised that his mum hadn't kept her promise, but he was still disappointed.

'You couldn't just keep your head down and your mouth shut, could you? You couldn't let Mum finish off in style. You had to go up there, scaring her half to death, making her feel guilty. But you don't care what anyone else wants. It's always about what *Jordan* wants and whatever the baby wants the baby gets.'

Jordan opened his mouth to try to defend himself, but Kyle didn't want to hear anything he had to say. 'Well, I hope you're satisfied. Just get off to school and try to keep out of trouble for once!'

Kyle nearly tore the bedroom door off its hinges before stamping downstairs. Jordan threw himself back on his bed. He clenched his fists and held back the tears. He would *not* cry and confirm his brother's opinion of him as an overgrown baby.

'You've got five minutes!' Kyle yelled again.

Jordan grabbed his clothes and dressed for school. He tried to drag his feet, hoping Kyle would go and leave him in the house, but when he went downstairs he found his brother standing by the back door in his coat with his workbag over his shoulder, waiting for him. Jet made a leap for Jordan and covered him with licks and kisses and, for a split second, Jordan felt the tears spring up again. At least somebody still loved him. He reached for Jet's lead but Kyle told him to leave it.

'The dog's been round the block. I did it, while you were still getting your beauty sleep. Here.'

Kyle handed Jordan a sandwich he'd also made earlier.

Jordan looked at it suspiciously. 'What's in it?' he asked.

'What d'you think, rat poison?'

Jordan took it and grabbed his jacket off the peg, picked up the end of a packet of biscuits and went out of the door. It was a heavy, grey sky, not yet raining but certain to later. He thought about going back to get his waterproof, but with Kyle almost steaming with anger behind him he decided not to bother. Kyle followed Jordan out, locking the door behind them.

Jordan turned and headed off down the road. When he stopped to look back, his brother was waiting at the gate, as if to see him completely off the premises before he left. These had probably been instructions from his dad that Kyle was following, but in his own obsessive fashion. When he saw Jordan looking back, he shouted, 'Just go, Jordan, and do us all a favour – don't come back.'

Kyle sometimes said things like that when he was in a temper; he was often harder on Jordan than his parents were. But for the first time Jordan felt as if Kyle might really mean it. He knew that his brother would now hold him personally responsible if their mum gave up early on her record. Jordan thought how, if she'd kept to the original plan, today would have been her first day home; but it was far too disappointing to dwell on.

Jordan's phone vibrated and his heart gave a little lurch when he saw that the text was from Anand. But as he read it, what he thought had been his lowest point just got even lower. '*Don't send me any more texts you traitor. Call yourself a friend. I'm finished with you!*'

This was the final straw for Jordan. There was no way he was going to school now. He couldn't face Anand and he didn't feel strong enough to face his tormentors again, especially now his best friend had taken their side and turned on him too.

It certainly wasn't the best day for fishing – the sky was full of weather, banking up as far as he could see – but he suddenly had a powerful need to be with his grandpa, or at least in a place where he could feel close to him. He turned back to get some warmer clothes – a waterproof and gloves certainly, and his Wellingtons – but when he felt in his jacket pocket he realised he hadn't got his key. It was still in his waterproof from last night. Jordan was so fed up with himself; of all the days to forget it. But there was nothing he could do now, so he buttoned his jacket to the neck, turned up his collar, and set off.

Jordan followed the riverbank, and stopped for a moment at his grandpa's bench, but it was far too cold to stay there. He went on picking his way through the mud, trying at first to keep his trainers clear of the worst of it, but after a while giving up the fight. He didn't go to his usual fishing spot; without his rod there was no point. He chose instead to leave the river and wander through the country park.

Over the last twenty years this whole area had been reclaimed from disused gravel pits and developed into a wildlife reserve, stretching from the centre of the city at one end, right out into the country at the other. It consisted of at least a dozen lakes that were now a magnet for migrating water birds.

Jordan headed down a particularly secluded path that he knew led to an almost-hidden stretch of the river, where it briefly doubled back on itself. You couldn't get to it by walking along the riverbank, because the path was inaccessible in places. There was a way to reach it, though, that he and his grandpa often used. He knew the exact spot to break through the dense shrubbery that would bring him onto a tiny almost-island. There was just enough space, if they sat close together, for him and his grandpa to set up their swims. They hadn't gone there often, because it wasn't the best place to fish, but they liked to think of it as their private place. So, when everyone had been discussing where to scatter his grandpa's ashes, it had seemed the obvious place to Jordan and he'd reluctantly decided to share it with the rest of his family.

It had been a cold February day and the wind was strong. Stan and Jacky, his grandpa's fishing friends, made a couple of jokes about not standing downwind – unless you wanted a mouthful of Billy. His gran hadn't been amused.

There had been over a dozen of them altogether: his gran, his mum and dad, sister and brother, aunt and uncle and his cousins, plus a handful of his grandpa's fishing pals. Jordan's mum was carrying the urn and had been about to shake out the ashes, but Jordan had stopped her. He'd had the presence of mind to realise they would all be blown away from the water into the trees, and none of them would end up in his grandpa's beloved river. So he'd led his mum to the edge and made her bend down low, holding onto her when she got nervous about falling in. He'd told her to tip the urn and slide the ashes out, just like his grandpa had taught him to return a fish to its swim – always making sure it was headed upstream so the water would wash over its gills and save the fish any extra distress.

Some of the ashes had still blown away, but most had settled on the surface, and they'd all stood in silence and watched them being carried away by the current. It made Jordan think of sailors being buried at sea, and he knew his grandpa would have been pleased with that – finally laid to rest in his beloved river.

He found himself crying now at the memory – there was no one to see him here, no need to feel embarrassed. He wished he'd brought something with him; he wasn't sure what, some fish bait maybe to throw on the water, like laying flowers on a grave. But Jordan shook his head. He didn't want to dwell on that thought. He was determined not to start thinking about his mum again this morning.

He quickly turned away from the river and headed back into the country park. With all the past week's rain, several stretches of the path were partly underwater. In the puddles Jordan tried to wash some of the mud off his trainers, but realised his mistake when the water came over the tops. His feet were properly wet now. He looked for a drier route, wishing again he'd got his Wellies on, and a warmer coat. The sky was a rich steely grey colour, both dark and light in places. The clouds looked bloated with rain, or snow – it was difficult to guess which.

He was deeper into the park now and meeting fewer and fewer people until he felt as if he had the place to himself. He walked with his head down and his hands in his pockets, kicking twigs and small branches out of his path. He looked up and suddenly saw a heron; not in or beside the water, as he usually saw them, but standing smack bang in the middle of the path. He'd never been this close to one before. He stood watching it for several moments, holding his breath.

He could see every detail. He gazed at its massive beak, imagining it diving for fish and spearing them with it. The heron looked back at him, or rather straight through him, as if it knew in that moment everything that was going on in Jordan's head, could understand his misery; might even, if it could speak, give him some words of advice.

Slowly Jordan advanced on it, with tiny silent steps, like he was playing Grandmother's Footsteps. At each step he expected the bird to fly, but the heron fixed him with its eye, as if issuing a direct challenge.

Jordan's heart suddenly skipped a beat as his phone vibrated. The heron looked at him almost wearily then rose with a minimum of effort, floating through the sky like a huge paper dart. Jordan watched it disappear behind some trees. There was nothing he'd have liked better right then than to sprout his own wings and fly after it, leaving all his problems behind.

He took out his phone and read the message from Martine. '*Where are you? Why aren't you in school?*'

He quickly replied. '*What's the point. Can't face it. Messed up big time.*'

Jordan couldn't bring himself to tell her anything about last night's monumental stupidity. So he put his phone away and pressed on, knowing that he needed to keep moving if he wanted to avoid completely freezing up. He walked for an hour or more, following the whole perimeter of the park until it brought him back to the river and at last to the weir. He walked onto the bridge that crossed over it. The river was so full it came rushing over the weir, carrying with it a disgusting collection of rubbish: fast-food cartons, bottles, paper, endless plastic bags. Lots of it had attached itself to the reeds around the riverbank, so that it looked like the scum round a bath that's in need of a good clean.

In complete contrast, the sheet of water that

tumbled over the weir almost gleamed, it was so clear and clean. Lots of water birds floated serenely along the far bank, away from the fast current. But one little duck caught up in it kept being drawn too close to the edge. Jordan leaned over the parapet and watched it paddling furiously to stay in the same place and avoid being carried over the weir. But despite its efforts, each time it got away the current dragged it back.

Jordan stayed and watched the bird for at least twenty minutes. He started to identify with the duck and imagine how exhausted it must be. In the duck's place he might just have given up and stopped paddling.

He was relieved when it reached a heap of twigs and rubbish that formed a little platform against the side of the bridge and hopped on top. But it had been a mistake, because now it was almost on the edge of the weir and would have to paddle twice as hard to get back to where it had been. Its only hope was to get up on the bridge. The duck kept bobbing up and down as if trying to gauge the jump it would need to reach the lowest ledge; its neck rose and fell as it made sort of practice moves.

'Go on, you can do it,' Jordan whispered, encouragingly.

The duck stopped, as if it were listening, then went back to bobbing up and down, like a bather on the side of a swimming pool who really wants to get in but suspects the water is cold. It went on bobbing for so long that Jordan could hardly bear it, but he couldn't drag himself away either. He felt as indecisive as the duck. It was making him angry, and he suddenly banged his fist on the bridge. The sudden movement caused the duck to turn and hop back into the water, where it started the business of furiously paddling all over again, then being drawn back ever nearer to the weir's edge.

'You stupid bird,' Jordan hissed at it and turned away in frustration.

It had been a mistake to stand still on the bridge for so long. His feet were almost throbbing, they were so cold. He thought of his grandpa's advice for cold hands, but sticking his feet in the freezing cold river seemed like some kind of torture. Instead, he stamped along the path, trying to get some feeling back.

The sky was deepening in colour, almost purple-grey now, and it seemed to be lower, as if the weight of rain – or snow – was dragging it down. He didn't know what to do next. He couldn't stay here for the rest of the day, getting colder and colder. He noticed how hungry he was, and no wonder; he realised it was nearly lunchtime. He took out the food Kyle had given him. The packet held two slices of toast with peanut butter; it had gone soft and a bit soggy, but he was so hungry he could hardly remember food tasting any better. It was gone far too quickly and left Jordan feeling even hungrier than before.

His phone began to ring. Almost simultaneously a text came through. He ignored the call – from his mum – but read Martine's text message: '*We're just getting out of school. We'll be round yours in a mo. Don't go anywhere!*'

Jordan shrugged. The '*we*' suggested Anand was with her, so he must have been in school. He briefly wondered what the story was, but he wasn't at all sure he was ready to face Anand – even if Anand wanted to see him.

Before Jordan could make any decisions, the sky turned even darker. In minutes it was sleeting, falling almost horizontally, stinging his face. He needed to find shelter, and he suddenly remembered where he could do that.

Jordan set off at a run.

CHAPTER TWENTY

Jordan headed back down the river, squelching through mud then sloshing through puddles, until his legs and feet were so wet he might as well have plunged them in the river. He could hardly see what was ahead of him because of the sleet in his eyes.

As he crossed a small humped-back bridge, he almost fell on the wet boards and twisted his ankle. The sudden twinge made him stop for a moment, but he pressed on, limping a bit, ducking round the end of the bridge onto a narrower path leading to a loop of the river, where a few people lived on houseboats. At the furthest end, as if the other boats were trying to distance themselves from it, was the one he was

263

looking for; the one his grandpa had nicknamed the *Marie Celeste*.

It was bigger by a long way than any of the other boats, and looked like a small bungalow floating on the river – at least, until it had started to sink. The boat was in very poor repair, but, according to his grandpa, had been lived in until a few years ago. It was abandoned now and slowly sinking lower in the water. Jordan used to bring Anand here, and the two of them had dared each other to jump on and off it. But the last time they'd given themselves too big a scare when the boat had almost capsized.

The two boys liked to pretend that when they grew up they would buy it; rescue it before it completely rotted away and live on it together. For some reason they'd never told Martine about the boat – it had been just their private place for a while.

Jordan was shocked to see the boat was sitting even lower in the water, maybe another ten centimetres since he'd last been here. When he looked through the windows, the water was no longer lapping round the legs of the table, but was now up to the seats of the chairs. Another ten centimetres and it would cover the tabletop.

Jordan hesitated; he wasn't at all sure the boat would take his weight, not without sinking dangerously lower. But the sleet was coming down even harder and he didn't really have a choice. He took the greatest care stepping on; even so, the boat lurched wildly and Jordan almost jumped off again. But he held onto a rail until it steadied and then rocked gently in the water.

He made for the small covered area where, if he squeezed himself in tight, he hoped he might just be sheltered from the worst of the weather. He crouched down and leaned against the door, puffing and panting as his breath – and his heart rate – slowed down. He felt relieved to be out of the rain and sat shaking and shivering for several minutes, his teeth literally chattering.

The first time his grandpa had shown Jordan the sinking boat, he'd told him the story of the *Marie Celeste* – a real ship with a captain and crew that was found abandoned with no sign of the ten people on board and no clue as to why they'd left the ship. It was one of those famous unsolved mysteries. A *regular ghost-ship*, his grandpa had called it, and the first time Jordan had brought Anand here he'd tried to frighten him by telling him the houseboat might be haunted too.

According to his grandpa's story, when the *Marie Celeste* was found, there was food and drink – still warm – on the table, and chairs cast aside as if the ship had been abandoned only minutes earlier. The houseboat had always seemed just the same to Jordan, because when he peered through the windows he could still see pots and pans in the galley-kitchen, as if someone had gone out one day and never come home, leaving all their belongings. The last people to live in it were a single mum with a couple of children, and one or two of their pictures were still on the walls. Jordan often imagined that some of their toys and other personal treasures might still be lying hidden under the water.

Jordan looked out from his hiding place and watched the river churn with the sheer force of the water pouring out of the sky, as if someone were emptying gigantic bucketfuls. This was what he imagined a monsoon would be like – but surely in countries where they had monsoons it would be a lot warmer than this.

He used his jacket sleeves to dry off his face and his hair, then wrapped his arms around himself. He was so *very* cold, and after the previous night, all he wanted to do was curl up and go to sleep. There was a tiny thought at the back of his mind that falling asleep might be a big mistake. Was it possible to develop hypothermia in half an hour, Jordan wondered, and perhaps never wake up again? It seemed a bit dramatic; it wasn't like he was in the Arctic, and anyway, his eyes were closing now of their own accord. Just as if someone was flicking a switch – one moment he was awake, the next he was deeply asleep.

He was in a boat swimming from room to room. He glided beneath a table, between chairs. Like an underwater Peter Pan, he swam through bedrooms, looking down through the water at children asleep in their beds with their teddies and dummies. There were toys and shelves full of books. It all looked so peaceful. He liked looking into the children's lives. He felt as if he knew them. When they woke up he could play with them on the boat, maybe show them how to fish from the deck.

He turned onto his back. Now he wasn't in the boat any more; he was floating on the surface of the river, the sun warm on his face. He could hear birds. He felt so happy he wanted to stay there all day – for ever if he could.

But after a while he began to feel lonely. He wanted the children to wake up and feel the sun on their faces. He flipped over in the water, intending to get back into the boat to waken them, but although he looked in all directions he couldn't see any sign of it. The boat had disappeared. It had sunk completely, while he wasn't looking, with the children still inside.

He started to dive – desperate to save them. He swam along the bottom, feeling with his hands when it became too dark to see anything, but he couldn't find the boat. It was as if the riverbed had opened up and swallowed it. He was starting to feel frantic; his lungs were bursting and he felt as if he might drown himself. But when he tried to get back to the surface, he found his legs were tangled with weed and rubbish. He kicked and kicked, desperate not to drown down there in the filthy clogged-up riverbed. He knew this one thing: he did not want to die...

Jordan woke panting and struggling for breath. What had woken him was the feeling that someone – or something – was poking him sharply in the arm. He saw that it was the tip of a long golfing umbrella.

'Wake up. Jordan, *wake up!*'

Jordan opened his eyes fully to see his two friends standing on the bank looking at him. They were almost as wet as him, despite the outsize golfing umbrella that Martine was now struggling to open again in the face of the driving wind and rain.

'What are you doing here, you idiot?' she asked, but Jordan was too sleepy to answer. 'You've got to get off this boat. It isn't safe. Come on,' she begged him. But Jordan simply couldn't. He'd been really cold lots of times when he'd been fishing, but nothing like this. His body felt as if it had gone into hibernation; it just wouldn't move. He closed his eyes and his head fell forward.

'Oh, my God, he isn't dead, is he?' Anand asked.

'Of course he's not dead, dummy. But he's not doing his health any favours. Come on, we've got to wake him up.'

Martine handed the umbrella to Anand and, putting one leg over the side of the houseboat, launched herself up on it. The boat rocked so much she stepped back to steady herself and ended up sitting on her bottom on the path.

'Do *not* laugh,' she warned Anand, who tried valiantly not to.

On her second attempt she managed to get on board and snatched back the umbrella. She looked impatiently at Anand.

'What are you waiting for?' she asked. 'A signed invitation?'

'I'm not going on there,' he announced. Anand was

clearly convinced that his weight might be the final straw that caused the houseboat to completely capsize.

'Look, if it'll take my weight it's not going to notice a seven-stone weakling like you. Now get on here,' she ordered him.

Anand finally took a nervous step over the side and immediately slid across the wet boards, ending up almost doing the splits. Martine reached out and helped him to his feet.

Jordan watched this little pantomime through half-open eyes. Martine struggled to hold onto the umbrella with one hand, while she carefully made her way to the shelter with the other. Anand edged his way behind her.

'Now you get hold of one arm,' she told Anand, 'and I'll get the other and we'll try to pull him up.'

Jordan found himself gripped by his two friends, then hauled up until he was standing. But the moment he put any weight on his ankle he yelped and promptly sat down again.

'Now what?' Martine asked impatiently.

'I sprained my ankle,' he mumbled.

'Great!' she announced. 'Just what we need.'

'Now what do we do?' Anand asked her.

'Well, there's no way we're going to carry him.'

Jordan struggled to keep his eyes open and focus on

270

his friends, who seemed like two phantoms from one of his dreams. He closed his eyes again, leaving them to work it all out. He felt so relieved that for once no one was asking him to fix anything.

'Get his dad on the phone,' Martine ordered. 'Tell him we've found him, but he'll have to come and help us get him home.'

'Yes, *sir*,' Anand said, sarcastically. Martine stood sheltering Jordan with the umbrella while Anand made the call. 'We've found him, Mr Gibbons. But he can't walk; he's broken his ankle.'

'Not broken it, for goodness' sake,' Martine hissed. 'You haven't broken it, have you?' she asked, anxiously.

Jordan shrugged. He didn't much care; he just knew he couldn't walk on it.

Anand explained exactly where they were then rang off. 'Now what?'

'Now we get out of the rain until they arrive,' Martine told him. 'Move over,' she told Jordan. 'And you sit on the other side of him,' she told Anand. She drew the umbrella around them, like drawing down a blind.

All three were tightly squeezed together so that it felt as if they were inside a small one-man tent. The driving rain beat on the umbrella and dripped a large puddle along the floor.

'I can hardly breathe,' Jordan moaned.

'There's no blooming room,' Anand agreed.

'Oh, stop complaining,' Martine told them. 'It's what you need – warming up – or you're going to get pneumonia,' she warned Jordan.

Anand was feeling more than uncomfortable. He was as upset as Martine to find Jordan looking like he'd been sleeping rough for a week, but he wasn't ready to forgive his friend and cosy up to him – pneumonia or not. But he was in no hurry to go back out into the rain either, so he settled back and tried to make the best of it.

'Everyone thinks you've run away,' he announced.

For the first time Jordan was interested. 'Why do they think that?'

Martine looked a little sheepish. 'Well,' she said defensively, 'when we couldn't find you round your house, we went up to see your mum…'

'Martine told her you hadn't been at school,' Anand said, smugly.

'I was worried,' Martine explained. 'Your text sounded a bit desperate, so…I thought you might have run away.'

Jordan groaned.

'Your mum called your dad and he organised a search party,' Anand added.

'A couple of people are out looking for you,' Martine corrected him.

'But I guessed where you'd be,' Anand said, looking pleased with himself.

'Yeah, how come you never told me about this place?' Martine asked.

'Boys' stuff,' Anand said, grinning at Jordan. Jordan managed a smile in return.

'Whatever,' said Martine, dismissively. 'So, what's the story?' she asked Jordan. 'What're you doing here?' But he still couldn't be bothered to go into the whole thing. He quite liked the idea that everyone had been worried about him for a change.

'I know what you need,' Anand announced, fishing in his pocket and bringing out a couple of KitKats.

Jordan hesitated and looked at his friend.

'It's OK,' he told him. 'They're not nicked.'

'Don't worry, he's learned that lesson,' Martine told Jordan. 'The hard way.'

Anand told him that his dad had made a big deal and banned him from playing football for a whole month – a serious punishment for Anand. 'But you know my old man, he'll have forgotten in a week,' he grinned.

'You hope,' Martine told him.

Jordan smiled and reached for the chocolate. 'You're a life-saver,' he told Anand.

'Yeah, well I think we've all earned a piece, don't you?' Martine added, helping herself to a finger.

When his dad and his Uncle Matt finally found them, they stood on the path, shaking their heads at the picture of the three kids under the umbrella. They shook their heads a whole lot more when they saw the state of Jordan.

'Oh, lad, what are we going to do with you?' his dad sighed. 'Come on, let's get you home. Can you get up?'

'I think you're going to have to lift him, Mr Gibbons,' Martine advised.

His uncle looked worried. 'Surely that boat's never going to take our weight.'

'We'll soon find out. You two better get off first,' his dad suggested, then he and his uncle nervously got on board. The whole boat seemed to bounce up and down for minutes before it steadied enough for them to attend to Jordan. His dad knelt down while he checked Jordan's ankle was only sprained and not broken. Then the two men lifted him to his feet. It took the four of them to get him off the boat and finally standing on one leg on the path.

Anand told them, proudly, 'It was me that found him, you know. I knew where to come.'

'Well, I don't want any of you coming back here from now on,' Jordan's dad told them. 'This is not a safe place to be playing, right?'

The three friends nodded and grinned. *Playing*. It made them sound like infants.

'I hope you know how lucky you are to have friends like these two,' his dad told Jordan.

Anand grinned even wider. He seemed to have forgotten all about feeling cross with Jordan.

'He sure is,' Martine agreed, modestly. 'Any more stunts like this and he won't be so lucky.'

With one arm round each of the men's shoulders, Jordan managed to slowly hop the few hundred metres to the car park. Martine walked close behind, trying to shelter them under the umbrella.

'Don't anybody worry about me,' Anand rabbited on, bringing up the rear. 'I'll just catch my death here.'

Jordan was put into the front seat of his uncle's car, while his dad sat in the back with Anand and Martine. Throughout the short drive home the car windows never cleared of condensation, as everybody and their clothes gently steamed. Jordan was wrapped in a car rug, and as he began to warm up he started to drowse again. He felt his dad shaking his shoulder.

'Don't go to sleep yet,' he told him. He pressed speed dial, then handed his phone over. 'Tired or not, you'd better speak to your mum. She's been out of her mind with worry, ever since Martine told her you hadn't been to school.'

It was answered in a moment.

'Hi Mum,' Jordan mumbled.

'Oh, thank God!' she breathed. 'Are you OK?'

'Mmm,' he told her, almost too tired to talk.

His dad took the phone back for a moment. 'Don't worry,' he said. 'He's wet, cold, dirty, smelly, and he's got a sprained ankle – apart from that he's fine. So, do you want to tell him, or shall I?'

'Tell me what?' Jordan asked, suddenly more awake.

Jordan's dad grinned and passed him back the phone. 'Christmas has come early, lad.'

CHAPTER TWENTY-ONE

Jordan slept for eighteen hours, only opening his eyes around midday on Thursday. When he finally did, and saw who was standing by his bed, he thought he must still be asleep and dreaming.

'What are *you* doing here?' he asked.

'That's not much of a welcome,' his gran told him. 'I'm looking after you; somebody had to. Now, are you ready for some chicken soup?'

Jordan seemed to eat from the moment he woke until his gran left that evening, by which time he felt happily stuffed for a change – or *pogged*, as his grandpa used to call it. She'd fed him soup and bread rolls and then rice pudding with brown sugar for his lunch. An hour later she'd brought him a piece of chocolate cake, and then at about four o'clock she'd appeared with some cheese scones, hot from the oven. He'd still managed to eat a big plate of stew for supper, followed by a piece of apple pie and custard. Later his dad had brought his own meal up on a tray and joined Jordan in his bedroom.

'I could have come downstairs,' he offered, but his dad told him he wasn't allowed out of bed for at least twenty-four hours.

On their way home the previous day he'd been checked over at the Health Centre. They'd sent Jordan home, but advised that he should have his ankle iced at intervals until the swelling went down. But his dad had been determined that Jordan get properly rested up after his little adventure. That night he stayed home with him, while Kyle did the full evening shift with his mum.

Jordan and his dad played Monopoly, and he had a feeling that his dad had let him win. As another special concession, Jet had been allowed upstairs to see him. But when Jordan asked if, *just this once*, the dog could sleep in his bedroom, his dad had told him, 'Don't push your luck, mate.'

Anand and Martine hadn't been allowed round to

visit, to make quite sure Jordan had as much rest as he needed, but there had been a regular stream of texts throughout the day. He was relieved that at least his friendships were back on track now.

He'd tried to explain to Anand that he'd never meant to get him in trouble with his dad, and that he was really sorry, but Anand clearly found Jordan's apologies embarrassing. He just wanted to forget it all, although he did remind Jordan yet again that a mint Christmas present might make up for it.

On Christmas Eve morning Jordan sat in the car with his dad as they drove up to the farm. Jordan wasn't looking particularly happy.

'For someone who's got exactly what he wants, you don't look on top of the world,' his dad told him.

It may have been the outcome Jordan had wanted, but it wasn't exactly how he had wanted it to be. Jordan hadn't wanted his mum to come out simply because everyone was worried about him. Even more than that, he didn't want it to be a complete anticlimax for her with no big party, no TV cameras, no newspapers. He didn't want to feel responsible for it being a letdown, after all she'd been through. But in the end she had decided to turn down the ten thousand pounds and the big exclusive in the newspaper.

'You don't want her to change her mind again, do you?' his dad asked, grinning.

But Jordan didn't want that either. He wanted her out in time for Christmas more than he'd ever wanted anything in his life. He just didn't want to be the one responsible – unless it really was what his mum wanted.

They'd talked about it for an hour last night, before he'd gone to sleep, and he'd asked her over and over, 'Are you absolutely sure, Mum?'

'Trust me,' she told him, 'I've had enough lying down to last me a lifetime. I'm stiff and sore and hurting all over. I can't wait to get out. I've done what I set out to do. The newspapers can keep their money.'

But he'd still pressed her. '*Really?*'

'Really, really, really,' she'd insisted. 'I'll see you tomorrow, sweetheart,' and the reality of those words had made them both almost cry.

When they arrived at the farm the diggers had been at work since eight o'clock and the hole was already a few metres deep. He was pleased to see that his aunt and uncle had hung huge banners everywhere saying

'*Welcome Home, Debbie, World Record Holder!*' Jordan felt guilty that he hadn't thought of doing something like that himself. He'd been stuck in bed all day yesterday with nothing to do and he hadn't even made her a measly 'Welcome Home' card. His cousins, Rosie and Ruby, bundled up in scarves and hats and mittens, were waving little flags, even though it might be an hour yet before his mum was actually out.

'This one's for you,' Ruby told Jordan. 'You have to wave it like this.' She demonstrated and Jordan, putting aside any worry about looking terminally uncool, waved his little flag in the air too.

There was a very festive feeling at the nursery, with Christmas carols being piped from the café. Lots of last-minute shoppers called at the farm shop for their holly wreaths, Christmas trees, and fruit and vegetables, and were waiting to see his mum actually come out. Plenty of friends and neighbours had turned up too, and nearly everyone seemed to be wearing Santa hats and holding up little banners or notices.

Jordan had expected to be given a bit of a hard time, so he was relieved to see everyone looking happy and relaxed, laughing and joking as his aunt handed out plastic cups of mulled wine. Even his brother seemed to have got over his temper. Kyle came over and messed up Jordan's hair, and for once Jordan didn't mind much.

'Here's the runaway,' Kyle laughed. Jordan could see Kyle was never going to let him hear the end of it. 'The only runaway to hitch a lift on a sinking boat.' His dad frowned, but it didn't stop Kyle.

'I *didn't* run away,' Jordan said calmly; he was determined not to get rattled today.

'Well, if you ever do,' Kyle warned him, 'make sure you take the dog with you next time. I've done all the dog walking this week and I'm sick of it.'

His aunt gave Jordan a hug. 'Take no notice,' she whispered. 'It's all over now.' She looked as relieved as he was. 'Do you want a chair, so you can rest that ankle?' she asked, but Jordan insisted he was fine. Today he didn't want any fuss around him.

Everyone was stamping their feet and trying to keep warm, which reminded his aunt how cold his mum would be when she came out. Jordan's dad was armed with his mum's heavy winter coat. There were a couple of paramedics standing by to give her a complete check over before she would be allowed to go home, but his aunt still couldn't stop fussing. 'I think I'll go and fill a couple of hot-water bottles, just in case,' she said.

Two cars pulled into the car park. Jordan recognised

the first as Ronnie King's. The reporter got out, accompanied by Colin the Camera. Jordan was surprised; he'd thought there weren't going to be any news people, now that his mum had cancelled her agreement with *The Weekend Sport*.

His dad shrugged. 'You didn't think we'd let her come out with nobody here to record it, did you?' Jordan could see now why Ronnie was looking *so* pleased with himself. This would be a big scoop for him.

The other car was his Uncle Matt's. His sister and her boyfriend were in the back seat and his gran in the front. Jordan felt a sudden rush of happiness as the three of them walked towards them. There was an awkward moment when Jordan wondered what everyone would do and say. He prayed there would be no arguments.

'Hello, Dad,' Chrissie said, a little awkwardly Jordan thought, but his dad stepped forward and gave her the kind of hug that almost took her breath away. They both looked close to tears. Even Kyle had gone a bit pink. Chrissie turned to Jordan. 'Hiya, little bro',' she said, grabbing him and also messing up his hair. Jordan beamed at her.

His gran was carrying a large Tupperware container. 'What you got there?' his dad asked, quickly wiping his eyes. 'Not more food for fattening up this little turkey?'

'Thanks, Dad,' said Jordan.

'They're not for him,' his gran sniffed. 'He could probably live for a week off what he ate yesterday. These are for Debbie. We all know the first thing she'll ask for when she gets out.'

Everyone laughed. His gran's mince pies were legendary and without question his mum's favourite food. She went off to heat some up in his aunt's oven, so they'd be ready for later.

More and more people had started to arrive; word must have got around. Jordan clearly wasn't going to get his quiet family reunion, after all, but he was in far too good a mood to mind about that. Ronnie was trying to organise everyone, telling them exactly how he wanted to set up *the big interview*. Even Colin the Camera was being unusually bossy.

'Can we move those cars out of the way? And is there anything we can do about that view? Those fields make a pretty depressing backdrop.'

'It's a farm,' his uncle muttered under his breath, 'and it's December. What does the fool expect?'

The diggers had almost finished their work, and when the first corner of the box appeared a huge cheer went up. Jordan limped forward to get a better view. The pipes hadn't been removed yet, and he couldn't wait for the moment when they were taken away and he would get the first glimpse of his mum.

Before that, though, the last of the digging needed to be done by hand. His dad, his Uncle Matt and Kyle all climbed down into the hole and started shovelling. When they were almost done his uncle climbed out and offered his spade to Jordan.

He was helped down the ladder and took up the spade. He'd never done a lot of digging, just the odd worm from the garden for fishing, and he didn't have much technique. But he did his best, clearing the area around the top pipe, while his dad and Kyle finished off the other end.

It was warm work, and Jordan stopped to loosen his jacket. He thought he could hear his mum's voice, and when he leaned closer he realised she was singing along with the carols. Jordan couldn't help smiling; his mum had a terrible singing voice – they were always teasing her about it. He was tempted to call down, 'Don't give up the day job, Mum,' but today it seemed like the best sound in the world.

Finally it was time to dismantle the pipes. His dad called down to warn his mum to keep away from the hole while they took the first one out. It was a tight fit and took a lot of wrenching, but it finally came away, and another *even bigger* cheer went up.

Jordan looked around, surprised at how many more people had arrived just in the time he'd been digging. There were more neighbours; friends of his mum's from work; people from school, including the two most important: Martine and Anand. They waved to him from the edge of the hole and Jordan waved back, grinning. Now everyone was here – everyone who mattered.

Once the pipe was gone there was nothing to stop Jordan from actually touching his mum. Colin the Camera got in position to take the first photo and zoomed in on Jordan as he knelt down and reached into the box. His stomach turned somersaults as he felt his mum grab hold of his hand. He forgot all the people that were there, watching him. 'I've missed you, Mum,' he whispered.

'Me too, darling, me too.'

While the last of the clearing up was done, and the second pipe was removed, Jordan talked with his friends, who were standing on the side of the hole. Martine bent down and passed him a Santa hat and offered him a mince pie, but Jordan was far too

286

excited to eat. He told her to give it to Anand, but he was already holding a mince pie in each hand.

Jordan shook his head. 'You little porker,' he said.

'That's his second lot,' Martine told Jordan, 'and we've only been here ten minutes.'

Further back in the crowd Jordan caught sight of Jason Carlisle and the Biscuit. His heart skipped a beat for a second, until he looked round at all his friends and family. He asked himself what on earth he had to be worried about, now that his mum was out, and they couldn't hurt her? What could they possibly do to him? He turned back and stared at the two boys, holding their gaze, until they finally acknowledged him. He wasn't scared of them and, what was more important, they knew that too.

Anand turned to see who Jordan was staring at. He shrugged and smiled. Perhaps life could get back to normal some time soon, Jordan thought. He turned back to watch his dad and Kyle using chisels as they started prising off the box lid.

For a while, Jordan had seriously believed that this moment might never come. At one low point, when he'd been especially 'mardy', according to Martine, she'd given him a bit of a talking to. 'You ought to realise how lucky you are. Your mum isn't dead, she's not seriously ill, she hasn't left you and gone off with someone else's dad. You're going to get her back. She's going to be coming home soon. Now stop feeling so sorry for yourself.'

To his shame Jordan hadn't listened to a word Martine had said, but now he could see his friend had been right. It had seemed a long time to have to wait, but here it was – his ordeal was *very nearly* over.

He heard the wood splintering as the nails gave way. Two sides were free, and a huge cheer went up, then a third – and another cheer. Finally, with only one nail still holding, his dad beckoned Jordan over to come and finish off opening the lid.

Martine called down to him, 'Don't you know it's bad luck to open your presents before Christmas morning?'

Jordan grinned and went over to join his dad.

'Happy Christmas, son,' he said, and put the chisel into Jordan's hands.